序 言

「初級英語聽力檢定①」出版後，受到讀者廣大的迴響，許多國中都集體訂購這本書，給了我們很大的鼓勵。

有人認為，增加聽力要多聽 ICRT、多聽空中英語、多看外國電影，這樣做，當然有助於聽力的訓練，但是，**做聽力試題，才是最直接有效的方法**，因為做題目的時候，才能使你專心聽，不專心聽，聽一輩子也沒有用。

「初級英語聽力檢定②」共有八份試題，由不同老師出題，Test 1 是由林銀姿老師負責，Test 2 和 Test 3，由張碧紋老師負責，Test 4 由蔡琇瑩老師負責，Test 5 由謝靜芳老師負責，Test 6 及 Test 8 由石支齊老師負責，Test 7 由蔡文華老師負責。由不同的老師命題，才能客觀，才容易命中考題。

考英語聽力是未來的趨勢，要加強聽力的直接方法，就是聽了再聽，要天天聽、常常聽，反覆練習。例如你起床後，你就可以把錄音機打開，走在路上可以一面走，一面聽，要聽習慣，聽多了，自然就會講，訓練聽力，也是練習會話的一種好方法，一石二鳥。

編輯好書是「學習」一貫的宗旨。本書在編審及校對的每一階段，均力求完善，但恐有疏漏之處，誠盼各界先進不吝批評指正。

劉 毅

全民英語能力分級檢定測驗
初級聽力測驗①

本測驗分三部份,全為三選一之選擇題,每部份各 10 題,共 30 題,作答時間約 20 分鐘。

第一部份: 看圖辨義

本部份共 10 題,試題冊上每題有一個圖片,請聽錄音機播出一個相關的問題,與 A、B、C 三個英語敘述後,選一個與所看到圖片最相符的答案,並在答案紙上相對的圓圈內塗黑作答。每題播出一遍,問題及選項均不印在試題冊上。

例: (看)

NT$80

NT$50

(聽)

Look at the picture. How much is the hamburger?

  A. It's eighty dollars.

  B. It's fifty-five dollars.

  C. It's eighteen dollars.

正確答案為 A

Question 1

Question 2

Question 3

Question 4

Question 5

Question 6

S	M	T	W	T	F	S
	1	2	3	4	5	6
7	8	9	10	11	12	13
14	15	16	17	18	19	20
21	22	23	24	25	26	27
28	29	30	31			

請 翻 頁 ⟹

Question 7

Question 8

Question 9

Question 10

請 翻 頁 ⫸

第二部份： 問答

本部份共 10 題，每題錄音機會播出一個問句或直述句，每題播出一次，聽後請從試題冊上 A、B、C 三個選項中，選出一個最適合的回答或回應，並在答案紙上塗黑作答。

例：

（聽） Good morning, Kevin. How are you?

（看） A. I'm fine, thank you.
　　　 B. I'm in the living room.
　　　 C. My name is Kevin.

正確答案爲 A

11. A. Couldn't be better.
　　B. Couldn't have been better.
　　C. I cook dinner for my wife.

12. A. All right.
　　B. You are welcome.
　　C. Thanks.

13. A. You failed the test.
　　B. Well done!
　　C. What a pity!

14. A. No, it's over there.
　　B. Yes, I need it.
　　C. Just this once. Remember to bring your own next time.

15. A. Help yourself.
    B. Cheers!
    C. Where is my tea?

16. A. We have a single
       room with a bath.
    B. Yes, there's enough
       room for one more
       on the back seat.
    C. No, there are no
       rooms for sale.

17. A. I had a sound sleep
       last night.
    B. I had a big meal
       yesterday.
    C. I didn't sleep very
       well last night.

18. A. He goes to work by
       MRT.
    B. He goes to work on
       time.
    C. He doesn't like to
       work at all.

19. A. Yes, it's the last stop.
    B. Yes, there will be
       another in five
       minutes.
    C. Which bus goes there?

20. A. Sorry to have kept you
       waiting.
    B. Never mind.
    C. Take it or leave it.

請 翻 頁 ◀▭⟹

第三部份： 簡短對話

本部份共 10 題，每題錄音機會播出一段對話及一個相關的問題，每題播出兩次，聽後請從試題冊上 A、B、C 三個選項中，選出一個最適合的回答，並在答案紙上塗黑作答。

例：

(聽) (Woman) Good afternoon, …Mr. Davis?

(Man) Yes. I have an appointment with Dr. Sanders at two o'clock. My son Tommy has a fever.

(Woman) Oh, that's too bad. Well, please have a seat, Mr. Davis. Dr. Sanders will be right with you.

Question: Where did this conversation take place?

(看) A. In a post office.

B. In a restaurant.

C. In a doctor's office.

正確答案為 C

21. A. Businessman and customer.

B. Husband and wife.

C. Two neighbors.

22. A. Turn down the TV because it's too loud.

B. Turn down the TV because it's too high.

C. Turn down the TV because it's too dark.

23. A. Teacher and student.
    B. Policeman and driver.
    C. Mother and son.

24. A. At 1:00.
    B. At 9:30.
    C. At 4:00.

25. A. A book.
    B. A watch.
    C. A doll.

26. A. She will get dressed before having breakfast.
    B. She will have breakfast first.
    C. She will have breakfast and get dressed at the same time.

27. A. She gets lost.
    B. She can't lend her notebook computer to the man.
    C. She doesn't need the notebook computer.

28. A. To a bathroom.
    B. To a post office.
    C. To a church.

29. A. Miss Lin looks much older than she is.
    B. Miss Lin doesn't look as old as she is.
    C. The woman doesn't know how old Miss Lin is.

30. A. At a toy store.
    B. At a library.
    C. At a restaurant.

初級聽力測驗詳解①

第一部份

Look at the picture for question 1.

  1.(**C**) What is Sam?

        A. He is a singer.

        B. He is a teacher.

        C. He is a cook.

        * cook〔kʊk〕*n.* 廚師

Look at the picture for question 2.

  2.(**A**) Who is the shortest girl?

        A. Jill is.

        B. Nell is.

        C. Gail is.

Look at the picture for question 3.

  3.(**C**) What are they doing?

        A. They are watching television.

        B. They are playing the piano.

        C. They are playing cards.

        * *play the piano* 彈鋼琴

        cards〔kɑrdz〕*n. pl.* 撲克牌遊戲

Look at the picture for question 4.

4. (**C**) What does Jane look like?
    A. She is a girl with long hair and glasses.
    B. She is a girl with short hair and sunglasses.
    C. She is a girl with short hair.

    * sunglasses〔'sʌnˌglæsɪz〕*n. pl.* 太陽眼鏡

Look at the picture for question 5.

5. (**B**) Where is the cat?
    A. It's in the box.
    B. It's between the box and the boy.
    C. It's in front of the box.

    * between〔bə'twin〕*prep.* 在～之間
    in front of 在～前面

Look at the picture for question 6.

6. (**A**) Today is January 3. What date is next Wednesday?
    A. It's January 10.
    B. It's January 3.
    C. It's January 17.

    * date〔det〕*n.* 日期

Look at the picture for question 7.

7. (**B**) What kind of ticket does Bob buy?
    A. He buys a movie ticket.
    B. He buys a train ticket.
    C. He buys an airplane ticket.

    * airplane〔'ɛrˌplen〕*n.* 飛機

Look at the picture for question 8.

8. (**A**) What is on sale right now?

      A. The air conditioner.

      B. The washing machine.

      C. The vacuum cleaner.

      * ***right now*** 現在   ***air conditioner*** 冷氣機

        vacuum〔'vækjʊəm〕*n.* 眞空

        vacuum cleaner 眞空吸塵器

Look at the picture for question 9.

9. (**B**) What time does the boy wake up?

      A. At ten o'clock.

      B. At noon.

      C. At six o'clock.

      * ***wake up*** 起床

Look at the picture for question 10.

10. (**A**) What does the symbol mean?

      A. Hand wash only.

      B. Do not iron.

      C. Do not wash.

      * symbol〔'sɪmbḷ〕*n.* 符號   mean〔min〕*v.* 意思是

        iron〔'aɪɚn〕*v.* 熨;燙

第二部份

11. (**A**) How are you doing today?
　　　A. Couldn't be better.
　　　B. Couldn't have been better.
　　　C. I cook dinner for my wife.
　　　* *Couldn't be better.*和 *Couldn't have been better.*
　　　都表示「再好不過了；好極了」。
　　　Couldn't be better. 好極了。（表示現在）
　　　Couldn't have been better. 好極了。（表示過去）

12. (**C**) The hat looks good on you.
　　　A. All right.
　　　B. You are welcome.
　　　C. Thanks.
　　　* *all right* 好的（表贊同）　　*You are welcome.* 不客氣。

13. (**B**) I got an A in English.
　　　A. You failed the test.
　　　B. Well done!
　　　C. What a pity!
　　　* fail〔fel〕*v.* 考試不及格　　*Well done*! 做得好！
　　　What a pity! 真可惜！

14. (**C**) Can I borrow your umbrella?
　　　A. No, it's over there.
　　　B. Yes, I need it.
　　　C. Just this once. Remember to bring your own next time.
　　　* borrow〔'baro〕*v.* 借（入）
　　　umbrella〔ʌm'brɛlə〕*n.* 雨傘·　　once〔wʌns〕*adv.* 一次
　　　this once 只此一次　　*next time* 下一次

15. (**A**)　Can I have a drink?

　　　　A. Help yourself.

　　　　B. Cheers!

　　　　C. Where is my tea?

　　　* ***help*** *oneself* 自行取用　　cheers〔tʃɪrz〕*interj.* 乾杯

16. (**B**)　Can you make room for me on the back seat?

　　　　A. We have a single room with a bath.

　　　　B. Yes, there's enough room for one more on the back seat.

　　　　C. No, there are no rooms for sale.

　　　* room〔rum〕*n.* 空間　　***make room for*** 爲～騰出空間

　　　back seat 後座　　single〔'sɪŋgl̩〕*adj.* 單人用的

　　　single room 單人房

　　　bath〔bæθ〕*n.* 浴室（= *bathroom*）　　***for sale*** 出售

17. (**C**)　What's wrong with you?

　　　　A. I had a sound sleep last night.

　　　　B. I had a big meal yesterday.

　　　　C. I didn't sleep very well last night.

　　　* ***What's wrong with you***? 你怎麼了？

　　　sound〔saund〕*adj.* 完全的；充分的

　　　a sound sleep 熟睡　　meal〔mil〕*n.* 一餐

18. (**A**)　How does David go to work?

　　　　A. He goes to work by MRT.

　　　　B. He goes to work on time.

　　　　C. He doesn't like to work at all.

　　　* MRT 大衆捷運系統（= *Mass Rapid Transit*）

　　　on time 準時　　***not～at all*** 一點也不～

19. (**A**) Does this bus go to the Taipei City Hall?
    A. Yes, it's the last stop.
    B. Yes, there will be another in five minutes.
    C. Which bus goes there?
    * *city hall* 市政府　　stop〔stɑp〕*n.* 站牌

20. (**C**) It's too expensive. Can't you make it cheaper?
    A. Sorry to have kept you waiting.
    B. Never mind.
    C. Take it or leave it.
    * expensive〔ɪkˈspɛnsɪv〕*adj.* 昂貴的
      Never mind. 沒關係。*Take it or leave it*. 要不要隨便你。

第三部份

21. (**C**) M：Hi, Alice! Your dog was making noise all night!
    W：I'm sorry, Leo. I'll keep him inside tonight.
    Question：Who are the speakers?
    A. Businessman and customer.
    B. Husband and wife.
    C. Two neighbors.
    * noise〔nɔɪz〕*n.* 噪音　　inside〔ˈɪnˈsaɪd〕*adv.* 在屋內
      neighbor〔ˈnebɚ〕*n.* 鄰居

22. (**A**) W：Tom! Turn the TV down!
    M：What? I can't hear you, Mom.
    Question：What does the woman mean?
    A. Turn down the TV because it's too loud.
    B. Turn down the TV because it's too high.
    C. Turn down the TV because it's too dark.
    * *turn down* 轉小聲（↔ *turn up* 開大聲）
      loud〔laʊd〕*adj.* 大聲的　　dark〔dɑrk〕*adj.* 黑暗的

23. (**B**) M：I have to write you a ticket because you made an illegal turn.

W：What? Are you kidding? I'm a law-abiding driver.

Question：Who are the speakers?

A. Teacher and student.

B. Policeman and driver.

C. Mother and son.

* ***write sb. a ticket*** 開罰單給某人　　***make a turn*** 轉彎
illegal〔ɪ'ligḷ〕*adj.* 違法的　　kid〔kɪd〕*v.* 開玩笑
law-abiding〔'lɔə,baɪdɪŋ〕*adj.* 守法的
driver〔'draɪvɚ〕*n.* 駕駛人

24. (**C**) M：Could I call on you this morning?

W：Sorry, I'm afraid not.

M：What time will be good for you?

W：Any time after three will be O.K.

Question： What time is the most convenient for the man to see the woman?

A. At 1:00.

B. At 9:30.

C. At 4:00.

* ***call on*** 拜訪（= *visit*）　　good〔gʊd〕*adj.* 合適的
convenient〔kən'vinjənt〕*adj.* 方便的

25. (**A**) M：What will you buy for Sandy's birthday?

W：Well, Sandy is fond of reading. Why don't we buy her something to read?

Question：What are they going to buy for Sandy?

A. A book.
B. A watch.
C. A doll.

* ***be fond of*** 喜歡（= *like*）

26. (**A**)　M：Are you going to dress first or have breakfast?
　　　　　　W：I'll get dressed right away.

Question：What will the woman do?

A. She will get dressed before having breakfast.
B. She will have breakfast first.
C. She will have breakfast and get dressed at the same time.

* dress〔drɛs〕*v.* 穿衣服　　***right away*** 立刻；馬上
at the same time 同時

27. (**B**)　M：May I use your notebook computer tonight?
　　　　　　W：I'm sorry, I need it.
　　　　　　M：Just tonight, OK?
　　　　　　W：No way!

Question：What does the woman really mean?

A. She gets lost.
B. She can't lend her notebook computer to the man.
C. She doesn't need the notebook computer.

* ***notebook computer*** 筆記型電腦
no way 不行　　***get lost*** 迷路
lend〔lɛnd〕*v.* 借（出）

28. (**B**) W：Where can I buy stamps?

M：Go straight on this street and turn left.

W：Thank you for your time.

M：You're welcome.

Question：Where is the woman going?

A. To a bathroom.

B. To a post office.

C. To a church.

* stamp〔stæmp〕*n.* 郵票　　straight〔stret〕*adv.* 筆直地
bathroom〔'bæθ,rum〕*n.* 浴室　　***post office*** 郵局
church〔tʃɝtʃ〕*n.* 教堂

29. (**B**) M：Miss Lin is 40 years old.

W：She doesn't look her age!　She looks about 30.

Question：What does the woman mean?

A. Miss Lin looks much older than she is.

B. Miss Lin doesn't look as old as she is .

C. The woman doesn't know how old Miss Lin is.

* ***look*** *one's **age*** 外貌與實際年齡相當
as…as ～　像～一樣…

30. (**A**) W：Ooh!　This bear is so cute.　It's a little girl teddy.
I'll take this one for myself.

M：If you like it, let me buy it for your birthday next week.

Question：Where are the speakers?

A. At a toy store.

B. At a library.

C. At a restaurant.

* bear〔bɛr〕*n.* 熊　　teddy〔'tɛdɪ〕*n.* 玩具熊（= *teddy bear*）
library〔'laɪ,brɛrɪ〕*n.* 圖書館

全民英語能力分級檢定測驗
初級聽力測驗②

　　本測驗分三部份，全為三選一之選擇題，每部份各 10 題，共 30 題，作答時間約 20 分鐘。

第一部份：　看圖辨義

　　　　　　本部份共 10 題，試題冊上每題有一個圖片，請聽錄音機播出一個相關的問題，與 A、B、C 三個英語敘述後，選一個與所看到圖片最相符的答案，並在答案紙上相對的圓圈內塗黑作答。每題播出一遍，問題及選項均不印在試題冊上。

例：（看）

NT$80　　　NT$50

（聽）
Look at the picture.　How much is the hamburger?

　　A.　It's eighty dollars.
　　B.　It's fifty-five dollars.
　　C.　It's eighteen dollars.

正確答案為 A

Question 1

Question 2

Question 3

Question 4

Question 5

Question 6

請 翻 頁 ⫸

Question 7

Question 8

Question 9

Question 10

請翻頁 ▥⟹

第二部份： 問答

本部份共 10 題，每題錄音機會播出一個問句或直述句，每題播出一次，聽後請從試題冊上 A、B、C 三個選項中，選出一個最適合的回答或回應，並在答案紙上塗黑作答。

例：

（聽）　Good morning, Kevin. How are you?

（看）　A.　I'm fine, thank you.
　　　　B.　I'm in the living room.
　　　　C.　My name is Kevin.

正確答案爲 A

11. A. Thank you, I will.
　　B. No, thanks. I'm very thirsty.
　　C. You're welcome.

12. A. Your watch is pretty good.
　　B. Better late than never.
　　C. I'm sorry. I don't have the time.

13. A. Yes, she looks very happy.
　　B. Don't worry. She just got too much sun today.
　　C. Yes, she doesn't look well.

14. A. Yes, I can.
　　B. Sorry, I'm not.
　　C. Of course I will.

15. A. Too late. It stopped
     ringing.
    B. I don't know how to do so.
    C. The line is busy.

16. A. It's not as beautiful as
     Mary's jacket.
    B. It's Johnny's.
    C. It's too warm to wear a
     jacket.

17. A. It really suits you.
    B. Of course you can give
     the suit to me.
    C. All right. I got it.

18. A. Would you like a
     chocolate shake with that?
    B. But you look so thin.
    C. Good idea. Salad is very
     fattening.

19. A. All right. Two
     heads are better
     than one.
    B. You're right. Too
     many cooks spoil
     the broth.
    C. Of course. Two's
     company, three's a
     crowd.

20. A. They will deliver it
     this afternoon.
    B. I'm so glad spring
     is here at last.
    C. You'd better take a
     sweater today.

請 翻 頁 ◖▭⟹

第三部份：　簡短對話

　　　　　　本部份共 10 題，每題錄音機會播出一段對話及一個相關
　　　　　　的問題，每題播出兩次，聽後請從試題冊上 A、B、C 三
　　　　　　個選項中，選出一個最適合的回答，並在答案紙上塗黑
　　　　　　作答。

　　　　　　例：

　（聽）(Woman)　Good afternoon, …Mr. Davis?

　　　　(Man)　　Yes.　I have an appointment with
　　　　　　　　　Dr. Sanders at two o'clock.　My
　　　　　　　　　son Tommy has a fever.

　　　　(Woman)　Oh, that's too bad.　Well, please
　　　　　　　　　have a seat, Mr. Davis.　Dr.
　　　　　　　　　Sanders will be right with you.

　　　　Question:　Where did this conversation take
　　　　　　　　　place?

　（看）A.　In a post office.
　　　　B.　In a restaurant.
　　　　C.　In a doctor's office.

　　　　正確答案爲 C

21. A. Yes, he does.
    B. No, he doesn't.
    C. I don't know.

22. A. She fell in love with
       a man.
    B. She lost her job.
    C. She got hurt.

23. A. No, he won't.
    B. Yes, he will.
    C. He is not willing to.

24. A. The woman did.
    B. The man did.
    C. John did.

25. A. Three minutes.
    B. Four minutes.
    C. Five minutes.

26. A. It isn't her day today.
    B. She fell out of her bed.
    C. She is fine.

27. A. It's fifteen to two.
    B. It's fifteen after one.
    C. It's one fifty.

28. A. The woman did.
    B. The man did.
    C. Another friend did.

29. A. He doesn't like his job.
    B. He doesn't like his
       co-workers.
    C. He doesn't like his boss.

30. A. No, he didn't.
    B. No, he hasn't.
    C. Yes, he has.

初級聽力測驗詳解②

第一部份

Look at the picture for question 1.

1. (**A**) How many apples are there in the tree?
   A. Four.   B. Five.
   C. Six.

   * ***How many~?*** 多少~?   ***in the tree*** (花、果實) 在樹上

Look at the picture for question 2.

2. (**C**) How is the weather?
   A. It is cloudy.   B. It is rainy.
   C. It is fine.

   * weather ('wɛðɚ) n. 天氣   cloudy ('klaʊdɪ) adj. 多雲的

Look at the picture for question 3.

3. (**B**) Where is the scarecrow?
   A. In the house.
   B. In front of the fence.
   C. Under a tree.

   * scarecrow ('skɛr͵kro) n. 稻草人   fence (fɛns) n. 籬笆

Look at the picture for question 4.

4. (**A**) What do you see in the sky?
   A. A rainbow.   B. A cloud.
   C. A typhoon.

   * sky (skaɪ) n. 天空   rainbow ('ren͵bo) n. 彩虹
   cloud (klaʊd) n. 雲   typhoon (taɪ'fun) n. 颱風

Look at the picture for question 5.

5. (**A**) What is the boy catching?
   A. He's catching butterflies.
   B. He's catching flies.
   C. He's catching mosquitoes.
   * catch〔kætʃ〕*v.* 抓　　butterfly〔'bʌtə͵flaɪ〕*n.* 蝴蝶
   　fly〔flaɪ〕*n.* 蒼蠅　　mosquito〔mə'skito〕*n.* 蚊子

Look at the picture for question 6.

6. (**C**) What are in the cook's hands?
   A. The chickens.
   B. The fish.
   C. The crabs.
   * cook〔kʊk〕*n.* 廚師　　chicken〔'tʃɪkən〕*n.* 雞
   　crab〔kræb〕*n.* 螃蟹

Look at the picture for question 7.

7. (**B**) What is the man doing?
   A. He's taking off his shoes.
   B. He's taking pictures.
   C. He's reading a novel.
   * ***take off*** 脫掉　　***take pictures*** 照相
   　novel〔'nɑvl̩〕*n.* 小說

Look at the picture for question 8.

8. (**C**) What's on the desk?
   A. There are some dishes on the desk.
   B. There is nothing on the desk.
   C. There are some donuts on the desk.
   * dish〔dɪʃ〕*n.* 盤子　　donut〔'do͵nʌt〕*n.* 甜甜圈

Look at the picture for question 9.

9. (**A**) Which is right?
   A. The boy is hammering.
   B. The boy is crying.
   C. The boy is making a cake.

   * right〔raɪt〕adj. 正確的　　hammer〔'hæmɚ〕v. 錘打
     cry〔kraɪ〕v. 哭　　***make a cake*** 做蛋糕

Look at the picture for question 10.

10. (**B**) What is the boy in the boat doing?
    A. He's sweating.
    B. He's rowing.
    C. He's waving.

    * boat〔bot〕n. 船　　sweat〔swɛt〕v. 流汗
      row〔ro〕v. 划船　　wave〔wev〕v. 揮手

第二部份

11. (**A**) Please have some more tea.
    A. Thank you, I will.
    B. No, thanks. I'm very thirsty.
    C. You're welcome.

    * have〔hæv〕v. 吃；喝　　thirsty〔'θɝstɪ〕adj. 渴的

12. (**B**) I'm sorry for being late.
    A. Your watch is pretty good.
    B. Better late than never.
    C. I'm sorry. I don't have the time.

    * late〔let〕adj. 遲到的　　pretty〔'prɪtɪ〕adv. 很；非常
      Better late than never. 【諺】遲到總比不到好。
      I don't have the time. 我不知道時間。

13. (**C**) She looks very pale.
    A. Yes, she looks very happy.
    B. Don't worry. She just got too much sun today.
    C. Yes, she doesn't look well.

    * pale〔pel〕 *adj.* 蒼白的　　worry〔'wɝɪ〕 *v.* 擔心
    sun〔sʌn〕 *n.* 陽光　　well〔wɛl〕 *adj.* 健康的

14. (**B**) Are you free on Friday?
    A. Yes, I can.
    B. Sorry, I'm not.
    C. Of course I will.

    * free〔fri〕 *adj.* 有空的　　*of course* 當然

15. (**A**) Please answer the phone.
    A. Too late. It stopped ringing.
    B. I don't know how to do so.
    C. The line is busy.

    * answer〔'ænsɚ〕 *v.* 接（電話）　　*stop* + *V-ing* 停止～
    ring〔rɪŋ〕 *v.* （鈴、鐘）響　　line〔laɪn〕 *n.* 電話線
    busy〔'bɪzɪ〕 *adj.* （電話）佔線的

16. (**B**) Whose jacket is this?
    A. It's not as beautiful as Mary's jacket.
    B. It's Johnny's.
    C. It's too warm to wear a jacket.

    * jacket〔'dʒækɪt〕 *n.* 夾克
    too…to～ 太…以致於不能～
    warm〔wɔrm〕 *adj.* 溫暖的

17. (**C**) Please give me a hand with this suitcase.
    A. It really suits you.
    B. Of course you can give the suit to me.
    C. All right. I got it.

    * ***give sb. a hand*** 幫助某人
      suitcase〔'sut,kes〕*n.* 手提箱
      suit〔sut〕*v.* 適合　*n.* 西裝　***I got it.*** 我知道了。

18. (**B**) Just a salad, please. I'm on a diet.
    A. Would you like a chocolate shake with that?
    B. But you look so thin.
    C. Good idea. Salad is very fattening.

    * salad〔'sæləd〕*n.* 沙拉　***on a diet*** 節食
      chocolate shake 巧克力奶昔
      thin〔θɪn〕*adj.* 瘦的
      fattening〔'fætənɪŋ〕*adj.* 使人發胖的

19. (**A**) Let's work together on this.
    A. All right. Two heads are better than one.
    B. You're right. Too many cooks spoil the broth.
    C. Of course. Two's company, three's a crowd.

    * ***work on*** 做；從事
      Two heads are better than one.
      【諺】三個臭皮匠，勝過一個諸葛亮。
      Too many cooks spoil the broth. 【諺】人多手腳亂。
      Two's company, three's a crowd.
      【諺】兩個人是伴，三個就嫌多。

20. (**C**)　The weather report said it is getting cold tonight.
　　　A.　They will deliver it this afternoon.
　　　B.　I'm so glad spring is here at last.
　　　C.　You'd better take a sweater today.

　　　* report〔rɪ'port〕*n.* 報導　　deliver〔dɪ'lɪvɚ〕*v.* 遞送
　　　at last 最後；終於　　*had better* 最好
　　　take〔tek〕*v.* 攜帶　　sweater〔'swɛtɚ〕*n.* 毛衣

第三部份

21. (**A**)　W：Do you smoke?
　　　M：Yes, I do.

　　　Question：Does the man smoke at all?
　　　A.　Yes, he does.
　　　B.　No, he doesn't.
　　　C.　I don't know.

　　　* smoke〔smok〕*v.* 抽煙　　*at all* 究竟

22. (**A**)　M：You are looking good.
　　　W：I fell in love with Ben.
　　　M：No wonder you are so busy these days.

　　　Question：What happened to the woman?
　　　A.　She fell in love with a man.
　　　B.　She lost her job.
　　　C.　She got hurt.

　　　* *fall in love with* 和～談戀愛　　*no wonder* 難怪
　　　these days 最近　　*happen to* 發生
　　　lose〔luz〕*v.* 失去　　job〔dʒɑb〕*n.* 工作
　　　get hurt 受傷

23. (**B**) W: Excuse me, would you please do me a favor?

M: Why not?

Question: Will the man help the woman?

A. No, he won't.

B. Yes, he will.

C. He is not willing to.

* ***do*** *sb.* ***a favor*** 幫忙某人　　***be willing to*** + *V.* 願意

24. (**C**) M: How did John learn English?

W: By watching the English programs on TV.

M: Maybe I can try the same way.

Question: Who learned English by watching TV?

A. The woman did.

B. The man did.

C. John did.

* program (ˈprogræm) *n.* 節目
the same way 相同的方式

25. (**C**) M: Can I help you?

W: The watch loses almost five minutes a day. I want
to have it checked.

Question: How many minutes does the watch lose a day?

A. Three minutes.

B. Four minutes.

C. Five minutes.

* lose (luz) *v.* (鐘、錶) 慢　　minute (ˈmɪnɪt) *n.* 分鐘
check (tʃɛk) *v.* 檢查

26. (**A**)　M：What's wrong with you?

　　　　W：Nothing. I guess I just got up on the wrong
　　　　　　side of the bed this morning.

　　　Question：What's the matter with the woman?

　　　A. It isn't her day today.
　　　B. She fell out of her bed.
　　　C. She is fine.

　　　* *It isn't her day today.* 她今天心情不好；她今天諸事不順。
　　　　get up on the wrong side of the bed 心情不好
　　　　fall〔fɔl〕*v.* 跌落（三態變化為：fall-fell-fallen）

27. (**B**)　A：Do you have the time?

　　　　B：It's one fifteen.

　　　Question：What time is it?

　　　A. It's fifteen to two.
　　　B. It's fifteen after one.
　　　C. It's one fifty.

28. (**B**)　M：Where did you go last night? I called you, but no
　　　　　　one answered the phone.

　　　　W：I went to the movies.

　　　Question：Who made the phone call?

　　　A. The woman did.
　　　B. The man did.
　　　C. Another friend did.

　　　* *answer the phone* 接電話
　　　　go to the movies 去看電影

29. (**C**) M : I'm going to quit my job.

W : Why?

M : I can't get along with my boss.

Question : Why is the man going to quit?

A. He doesn't like his job.

B. He doesn't like his co-workers.

C. He doesn't like his boss.

* quit〔kwɪt〕v. 辭職

get along with *sb.* 與某人和睦相處

boss〔bɔs〕*n.* 老板　　co-worker〔ko'wɜkə〕*n.* 同事

30. (**B**) W : Don't forget to wash the dishes.

M : OK. I'll do it later.

Question : Has the man washed the dishes?

A. No, he didn't.

B. No, he hasn't.

C. Yes, he has.

* later〔'letə〕*adv.* 待會兒；後來

【劉毅老師的話】

聽錄音帶的時候，要先看選項，再聽，萬
一有一條題目沒聽懂，馬上放棄，看下一
題的選項，看題目要領先，才容易得分。

全民英語能力分級檢定測驗
初級聽力測驗③

　　本測驗分三部份，全為三選一之選擇題，每部份各 10 題，共 30 題，作答時間約 20 分鐘。

第一部份： 看圖辨義
　　　　　本部份共 10 題，試題冊上每題有一個圖片，請聽錄音機播出一個相關的問題，與 A、B、C 三個英語敘述後，選一個與所看到圖片最相符的答案，並在答案紙上相對的圓圈內塗黑作答。每題播出一遍，問題及選項均不印在試題冊上。

例：（看）

NT$80　　NT$50

（聽）

Look at the picture.　How much is the hamburger?

　　A.　It's eighty dollars.
　　B.　It's fifty-five dollars.
　　C.　It's eighteen dollars.

正確答案為 A

Question 1

Question 2

Question 3

Question 4

To\Train	188	215	629
Taipei	06:03	07:00	08:30
Keelung	06:43	--:--	09:15
Ilan	08:10	09:00	10:55

Question 5

John = Ann

Sue   Tom = Cathy

Question 6

MONICA'S CAFÉ

Open 10:00am~10:00pm
$299 for each meal
301 Main St.
Tel:555-1905

請 翻 頁 ◀▭⟹

Question 7

Question 8

	SUN	MON	TUE	WED	THU	FRI	SAT	
Morning								
Afternoon			BOOK		BOOK		BOOK	
Evening	BOOK		BOOK		BOOK			

Question 9

Question 10

請翻頁 ▯◻⟹

第二部份： 問答

本部份共 10 題，每題錄音機會播出一個問句或直述句，
每題播出一次，聽後請從試題冊上 A、B、C 三個選項中，
選出一個最適合的回答或回應，並在答案紙上塗黑作答。

例：

（聽） Good morning, Kevin. How are you?

（看） A. I'm fine, thank you.
B. I'm in the living room.
C. My name is Kevin.

正確答案為 A

11. A. He gave me an
operation.
B. He told me to take it easy.
C. He shot me.

12. A. Where did you see it last?
B. Where did you buy
your coat?
C. Where is the
dictionary?

13. A. She is thirty.
B. Forty kilograms.
C. She cannot wait.

14. A. You are very kind.
B. I'm sorry. I didn't
get you anything.
C. Same to you.

15. A. You must be very
　　　proud.
　　B. Thank you. It's nice
　　　to meet you, too.
　　C. You're welcome.

16. A. Let's leave in July.
　　B. Let's go abroad.
　　C. Let's go skiing in
　　　Japan.

17. A. I eat three meals a day.
　　B. The supermarket is
　　　open.
　　C. I like Chinese food
　　　best.

18. A. I've had this cold
　　　since yesterday.
　　B. No, I couldn't hear
　　　him.
　　C. No, he threw it too
　　　fast.

19. A. John is liked by
　　　everyone.
　　B. There are more
　　　students in my class.
　　C. That's a popular idea.

20. A. By nine o'clock.
　　B. I rode my bike.
　　C. My home is far away.

請 翻 頁 ‖⟹

第三部份：　簡短對話

本部份共 10 題，每題錄音機會播出一段對話及一個相關的問題，每題播出兩次，聽後請從試題冊上 A、B、C 三個選項中，選出一個最適合的回答，並在答案紙上塗黑作答。

例：

（聽）(Woman)　Good afternoon, …Mr. Davis?

(Man)　　　Yes.　I have an appointment with Dr. Sanders at two o'clock.　My son Tommy has a fever.

(Woman)　Oh, that's too bad.　Well, please have a seat, Mr. Davis.　Dr. Sanders will be right with you.

Question:　Where did this conversation take place?

（看）A.　In a post office.

B.　In a restaurant.

C.　In a doctor's office.

正確答案為 C

21. A. In a bank.
    B. In a market.
    C. In a restaurant.

22. A. Her glasses.
    B. Her book.
    C. A new table.

23. A. 3:00.
    B. 6:30.
    C. 12:30.

24. A. Stay at home.
    B. Call his mother.
    C. Buy a present.

25. A. Chinese restaurant.
    B. Italian restaurant.
    C. Fast-food restaurant.

26. A. Call Mr. Brown.
    B. Call John.
    C. Give Mr. Brown a message.

27. A. A large red jacket.
    B. A large blue jacket.
    C. A large green jacket.

28. A. It walked off the table.
    B. It fell to the floor.
    C. The woman took it.

29. A. Listening to music.
    B. Talking on the telephone.
    C. Carrying a radio.

30. A. The woman's bicycle.
    B. The woman's leg.
    C. The woman's coat.

初級聽力測驗詳解③

第一部份

Look at the picture for question 1.

1. (**B**) What are they playing on?
   A. They are playing on a swing.
   B. They are playing on a seesaw.
   C. They are playing on a jungle gym.

   * swing〔swɪŋ〕 *n.* 鞦韆　　seesaw〔'si,sɔ〕 *n.* 蹺蹺板
   jungle gym 立體方格鐵架（兒童遊戲用）

Look at the picture for question 2.

2. (**A**) Where are the children?
   A. On the playground.
   B. In the department store.
   C. At the bus station.

   * playground〔'ple,graʊnd〕 *n.* 運動場；遊樂場

Look at the picture for question 3.

3. (**C**) What are they playing?
   A. The girl is playing the guitar and the boy is playing the violin.
   B. The girl is playing the piano and the boy is playing the drums.
   C. The girl is playing the piano and the boy is playing the guitar.

   * guitar〔gɪ'tɑr〕 *n.* 吉他　　violin〔,vaɪə'lɪn〕 *n.* 小提琴
   piano〔pɪ'æno〕 *n.* 鋼琴　　drum〔drʌm〕 *n.* 鼓

Look at the picture for question 4.

4. (**B**) I am in Taipei. I missed the 6:03 train. What train should I take?
   A. 188.
   B. 215.
   C. 629.

   * miss〔mɪs〕v. 錯過
     Keelung 基隆　***Ilan*** 宜蘭

Look at the picture for question 5.

5. (**B**) Who's John and Ann's daughter?
   A. Cathy is.
   B. Sue is.
   C. Tom is.

   * daughter〔'dɔtɚ〕n. 女兒

Look at the picture for question 6.

6. (**C**) How many hours a day is the shop open?
   A. Ten hours.
   B. Eleven hours.
   C. Twelve hours.

   * café〔kə'fe〕n. 咖啡廳　　meal〔mil〕n. 一餐
     hour〔aʊr〕n. 小時　　shop〔ʃɑp〕n. 商店
     open〔'opən〕adj. 營業的

Look at the picture for question 7.

7. (**A**) What is the girl holding?
   A. A teddy bear.
   B. A toy car.
   C. A jump rope.

   * hold〔hold〕*v.* 抱　　***teddy bear*** 泰迪熊；玩具熊
   toy car 玩具車　　***jump rope*** 跳繩

Look at the picture for question 8.

8. (**B**) When do you have a dancing class?
   A. On Sunday afternoon.
   B. On Tuesday evening.
   C. On Saturday.

   * ***dancing class*** 舞蹈課

Look at the picture for question 9.

9. (**A**) Why is the boy wearing a helmet?
   A. He's riding a skateboard.
   B. He's playing in the sand.
   C. He's playing at school.

   * helmet〔'hɛlmɪt〕*n.* 安全帽
   skateboard〔'sket,bord〕*n.* 滑板
   ride a skateboard 溜滑板
   sand〔sænd〕*n.* 沙

Look at the picture for question 10.

10. (**A**) What can you see in the circus?

    A. A clown.

    B. A cow.

    C. A bench.

    * circus ('sɜkəs) *n.* 馬戲團   clown (klaun) *n.* 小丑

    cow (kau) *n.* 母牛   bench (bɛntʃ) *n.* 長椅

第二部份

11. (**B**) What did the doctor say?

    A. He gave me an operation.

    B. He told me to take it easy.

    C. He shot me.

    * doctor ('dɑktɚ) *n.* 醫生

    operation (ˌɑpə'reʃən) *n.* 手術

    take it easy 放輕鬆

    shoot (ʃut) *v.* (開槍) 射中 (三態變化為：shoot-shot-shot)

12. (**C**) Please look up the word "overcoat."

    A. Where did you see it last?

    B. Where did you buy your coat?

    C. Where is the dictionary?

    * *look up* 查閱   overcoat ('ovɚˌkot) *n.* 外套；大衣

    last (læst) *adv.* 上一次

    dictionary ('dɪkʃənˌɛrɪ) *n.* 字典

13. (**B**) How much does your daughter weigh?
     A. She is thirty.
     B. Forty kilograms.
     C. She cannot wait.

     * *How much*~? 多少~？（接不可數名詞）
     weigh〔we〕*v.* 重~
     kilogram〔'kɪləˌgræm〕*n.* 公斤
     cannot wait 等不及

14. (**A**) Happy birthday! Here is a present for you.
     A. You are very kind.
     B. I'm sorry. I didn't get you anything.
     C. Same to you.

     * present〔'prɛznt〕*n.* 禮物
     kind〔kaɪnd〕*adj.* 體貼的
     get〔gɛt〕*v.* 買給~
     Same to you. 你也是。(= *The same to you.*)

15. (**B**) It's an honor to meet you.
     A. You must be very proud.
     B. Thank you. It's nice to meet you, too.
     C. You're welcome.

     * honor〔'ɑnɚ〕*n.* 榮幸   meet〔mit〕*v.* 認識
     proud〔praʊd〕*adj.* 驕傲的

16. (**B**) Where shall we go for the summer holiday?

  A. Let's leave in July.

  B. Let's go abroad.

  C. Let's go skiing in Japan.

   * leave〔 liv 〕*v.* 離開 *go abroad* 出國

   go skiing 滑雪

17. (**C**) What kind of food do you like to eat?

  A. I eat three meals a day.

  B. The supermarket is open.

  C. I like Chinese food best.

   * kind〔 kaɪnd 〕*n.* 種類

   three meals a day 一天三餐

   supermarket〔'supɚ,markɪt 〕*n.* 超級市場

18. (**B**) Did you catch what he said?

  A. I've had this cold since yesterday.

  B. No, I couldn't hear him.

  C. No, he threw it too fast.

   * catch〔 kætʃ 〕*v.* 了解 cold〔 kold 〕*n.* 感冒

   hear〔 hɪr 〕*v.* 聽到 throw〔 θro 〕*v.* 丟

19. (**A**) Who is the most popular student in your class?

  A. John is liked by everyone.

  B. There are more students in my class.

  C. That's a popular idea.

   * popular〔'papjəlɚ 〕*adj.* 受歡迎的；流行的；普遍的

   idea〔 aɪ'diə 〕*n.* 主意；想法

20. (**B**)　How did you come home yesterday?

A. By nine o'clock.

B. I rode my bike.

C. My home is far away.

* by〔baɪ〕*prep.* 在～之前　　***far away*** 很遠

第三部份

21. (**B**)　W：How much are your apples?

M：Nine dollars a pound.

W：Oh!　That's too expensive.

Question：Where are the speakers?

A. In a bank.

B. In a market.

C. In a restaurant.

* pound〔paʊnd〕*n.* 磅（重量單位）

expensive〔ɪk'spɛnsɪv〕*adj.* 昂貴的

bank〔bæŋk〕*n.* 銀行　　market〔'mɑrkɪt〕*n.* 市場

22. (**A**)　W：Please hand me my glasses.

M：Where are they?

W：On the table, next to the green book.

Question：What does the woman want?

A. Her glasses.

B. Her book.

C. A new table.

* hand〔hænd〕*v.* 傳遞　　glasses〔'glæsɪz〕*n. pl.* 眼鏡

next to 在～旁邊

23. (**C**)　M：Excuse me.　When is the next bus for Taichung?

W：Not until three thirty.

M：Oh, no!　I have to wait three hours?

Question：What time is it now?

A. 3:00.

B. 6:30.

C. 12:30.

* wait〔wet〕*v.* 等

24. (**C**)　W：Let's go shopping.

M：I'd rather not.

W：But Mother's Day is just around the corner.

M：Oh, then I had better go.

Question：What will the man do?

A. Stay at home.

B. Call his mother.

C. Buy a present.

* ***would rather*** 寧願（縮寫為'd rather）

Mother's Day 母親節

corner〔'kɔrnɚ〕*n.* 角落；轉角

around the corner 即將來臨

had better ＋V. 最好　　stay〔ste〕*v.* 待；停留

25. (**B**)　M：Are you ready to order?
　　　　　　W：Yes, we'll have an order of spaghetti, a cheese
　　　　　　　　pizza, and some white wine.

　　　　　Question：What kind of restaurant is it?
　　　　　A.　Chinese restaurant.
　　　　　B.　Italian restaurant.
　　　　　C.　Fast-food restaurant.

　　　　＊ order〔'ɔrdɚ〕v. 點菜　n.（食物的）一份
　　　　　　spaghetti〔spə'gɛtɪ〕n. 義大利麵
　　　　　　cheese〔tʃiz〕n. 乳酪
　　　　　　pizza〔'pitsə〕n. 披薩　　wine〔waɪn〕n. 葡萄酒
　　　　　　white wine 白酒　　**Italian**〔ɪ'tæljən〕adj. 義大利的
　　　　　　fast-food〔'fæst 'fud〕adj. 速食的

26. (**C**)　M：May I speak to Mr. Brown?
　　　　　　W：I'm sorry he's out.　Can I take a message?
　　　　　　M：Yes.　Please tell him to call John.

　　　　　Question：What will the woman do?
　　　　　A.　Call Mr. Brown.
　　　　　B.　Call John.
　　　　　C.　Give Mr. Brown a message.

　　　　＊ message〔'mɛsɪdʒ〕n. 訊息；留言
　　　　　　take a message 為～留言；傳話

27. (**B**)　W：Do you have this jacket in a large?
　　　　　　M：Yes, but only in blue.
　　　　　　W：Oh, that's too bad.　I prefer red.

Question: What does the man have?

A. A large red jacket.

B. A large blue jacket.

C. A large green jacket.

* jacket〔ˊdʒækɪt〕n. 夾克

large〔lɑrdʒ〕n. 大尺寸　adj. 大號的

prefer〔prɪˊfɝ〕v. 比較喜歡

28. (**B**)　M：Did you take my pen?

W：No, of course not.

M：Then where is it? It couldn't have just walked away.

W：Look. It's under your chair.

Question: What happened to the pen?

A. It walked off the table.

B. It fell to the floor.

C. The woman took it.

* take〔tek〕v. 拿走　　***walk away*** 走開

walk off 從~走開　　fall〔fɔl〕v. 掉落

floor〔flor〕n. 地板

29. (**B**)　W：Please turn down the radio.

M：Why?

W：I'm on the telephone.

Question: What is the woman doing?

A. Listening to music.

B. Talking on the telephone.

C. Carrying a radio.

* ***turn down*** 關小聲　　***on the telephone*** 講電話

carry〔ˊkærɪ〕v. 攜帶；提著

30. (**B**) M: What happened to your leg?

W: I had a bike accident yesterday.

M: Is it broken?

W: I'm afraid so.

Question: What is broken?

A. The woman's bicycle.

B. The woman's leg.

C. The woman's coat.

* ***What happened to～*** ? ～怎麼了？
  accident〔'æksədənt〕*n.* 意外；車禍
  broken〔'brokən〕*adj.* 骨折的；故障的
  I'm afraid so. 恐怕是如此。

【劉毅老師的話】

訓練聽力最好的方法，就是不停地做題
目，做了再做，平時早上一起來就可以把
錄音機打開，一面穿衣服就可以一面聽，
一面洗澡，也可以一面聽。

全民英語能力分級檢定測驗
初級聽力測驗④

　　本測驗分三部份，全爲三選一之選擇題，每部份各 10 題，共 30 題，作答時間約 20 分鐘。

第一部份： 看圖辨義

　　　　　本部份共 10 題，試題冊上每題有一個圖片，請聽錄音機播出一個相關的問題，與 A、B、C 三個英語敘述後，選一個與所看到圖片最相符的答案，並在答案紙上相對的圓圈內塗黑作答。每題播出一遍，問題及選項均不印在試題冊上。

例：（看）

NT$80　　NT$50

（聽）

Look at the picture.　How much is the hamburger?

　　A.　It's eighty dollars.
　　B.　It's fifty-five dollars.
　　C.　It's eighteen dollars.

正確答案爲 A

Question 1

	MON	TUE	WED	THU	FRI
1	CHINESE	ENGLISH	MATH	ENGLISH	GEOGRAPHY
2	MUSIC	CHINESE	GEOGRAPHY	MATH	CHINESE
3	MATH	FINE ARTS	P. E.	HISTORY	ENGLISH
4	P. E.	HISTORY	ENGLISH	CHINESE	MATH

Question 2

$20 $40 $25

Question 3

Question 4

Question 5

Question 6

請翻頁 ⫸

Question 7

Nancy   Jenny   Mary

Question 8

Question 9

Question 10

請翻頁 ▯◻⟹

第二部份：問答

　　本部份共 10 題，每題錄音機會播出一個問句或直述句，每題播出一次，聽後請從試題冊上 A、B、C 三個選項中，選出一個最適合的回答或回應，並在答案紙上塗黑作答。

例：

（聽）　Good morning, Kevin. How are you?

（看）　A.　I'm fine, thank you.
　　　　B.　I'm in the living room.
　　　　C.　My name is Kevin.

　　　　正確答案為 A

11. A. Wow! They are beautiful.
　　B. Really? Good for you!
　　C. Oh, I forgot to water them.

12. A. Sure. What do you need?
　　B. Sure. Here you are.
　　C. Sure. I give up.

13. A. I was born in Taipei.
　　B. I was born in winter.
　　C. I was born in November.

14. A. You had better wear your coat.
　　B. What a beautiful sweater!
　　C. Wow! They are really cool.

15. A. I enjoy watching TV.
    B. I like to listen to
       popular music.
    C. I love basketball.

16. A. 11:30.
    B. 11:15.
    C. 11:10.

17. A. She should wear a
       pair of glasses.
    B. She should wear a
       watch.
    C. She should wear
       a hat.

18. A. See you later.
    B. See you on Monday.
    C. Wait and see.

19. A. The doctor.
    B. The mailman.
    C. The neighbor.

20. A. I was lucky to catch
       them.
    B. They were easy. I
       think I passed them
       all.
    C. All of us had a good
       time today.

請 翻 頁 ⬛⟹

第三部份： 簡短對話

本部份共 10 題，每題錄音機會播出一段對話及一個相關
的問題，每題播出兩次，聽後請從試題冊上 A、B、C 三
個選項中，選出一個最適合的回答，並在答案紙上塗黑
作答。

例：

(聽) (Woman) Good afternoon, …Mr. Davis?

(Man)   Yes. I have an appointment with Dr. Sanders at two o'clock. My son Tommy has a fever.

(Woman) Oh, that's too bad. Well, please have a seat, Mr. Davis. Dr. Sanders will be right with you.

Question: Where did this conversation take place?

(看) A. In a post office.

B. In a restaurant.

C. In a doctor's office.

正確答案為 C

21. A. Come near him.
    B. Take away the puppy.
    C. Buy the puppy.

22. A. He thinks he has a cold.
    B. He also thinks it is better to close the window.
    C. He doesn't want the woman to close the window.

23. A. Wife and husband.
    B. Mother and son.
    C. Sister and brother.

24. A. She is afraid of the cake.
    B. She is afraid of getting lost.
    C. She is afraid of gaining weight.

25. A. She doesn't know the man.
    B. She doesn't know where the theater is, either.
    C. She doesn't want to tell him where the theater is.

26. A. He is too busy to wash the window.
    B. The window is too dirty to be washed clean.
    C. The window should be cleaned once a week.

27. A. To send some letters.
    B. To buy some stamps.
    C. To collect her mail.

28. A. He thinks it's a great one.
    B. He was sleeping and didn't finish watching the movie.
    C. He doesn't think it's good.

29. A. He eats a lot.
    B. He eats a little.
    C. He eats little.

30. A. Tom should buy a new typewriter.
    B. Tom shouldn't write to a pen pal.
    C. Tom has poor handwriting.

初級聽力測驗詳解④

第一部份

Look at the picture for question 1.

1. (**C**) How many math classes does John have every week?
   A. One class.
   B. Two classes.
   C. Four classes.

   * ***class schedule*** 課表　　math〔 mæθ 〕*n.* 數學
     PE 體育（ = *physical education* ）
     fine arts 美術　　history〔'hɪstrɪ 〕*n.* 歷史
     geography〔 dʒi'ɑgrəfɪ 〕*n.* 地理

Look at the picture for question 2.

2. (**B**) How much did Jack spend for his breakfast?
   A. 80 dollars.
   B. 85 dollars.
   C. 90 dollars.

Look at the picture for question 3.

3. (**A**) What are the ducks doing?
   A. They are swimming.
   B. They are eating.
   C. They are flying.

   * duck〔 dʌk 〕*n.* 鴨子　　fly〔 flaɪ 〕*v.* 飛

Look at the picture for question 4.

4. (**C**)　What does Mr. Smith order for dinner?
　　　　　A. He orders a hamburger and a coke.
　　　　　B. He orders a piece of pie and juice.
　　　　　C. He orders a steak and wine.

　　　　　* order〔'ɔrdɚ〕v. 點菜　　juice〔dʒus〕n. 果汁
　　　　　　steak〔stek〕n. 牛排　　wine〔waɪn〕n. 葡萄酒

Look at the picture for question 5.

5. (**B**)　What is the lady using?
　　　　　A. She is using a computer.
　　　　　B. She is using a cell phone.
　　　　　C. She is using a pay phone.

　　　　　* *cell phone* 大哥大；手機　　*pay phone* 公共電話

Look at the picture for question 6.

6. (**B**)　What does Jenny enjoy when she is free?
　　　　　A. She enjoys running.
　　　　　B. She enjoys dancing.
　　　　　C. She enjoys reading.

　　　　　* free〔fri〕adj. 有空的

Look at the picture for question 7.

7. (**C**)　Which description best matches the picture?
　　　　　A. Mary is the girl with short straight hair.
　　　　　B. Jenny is the girl with long straight hair.
　　　　　C. Nancy is the girl with short curly hair.

　　　　　* description〔dɪ'skrɪpʃən〕n. 描述
　　　　　　match〔mætʃ〕v. 符合　　straight〔stret〕adj. 直的
　　　　　　curly〔'kɝlɪ〕adj. 捲的

Look at the picture for question 8.

8. (**A**)　What is Helen dressing up for?
　　　A. For a party.
　　　B. For a concert.
　　　C. For a picnic.
　　　* *what…for*?　為什麼～?（= *why*～?）
　　　　dress up 盛裝打扮　　concert（'kɑnsɝt）*n.* 音樂會

Look at the picture for question 9.

9. (**C**)　Peter is thirsty now.　What does he want to drink?
　　　A. A beer.
　　　B. A cup of coffee.
　　　C. A glass of water.
　　　* thirsty（'θɝstɪ）*adj.* 口渴的　　beer（bɪr）*n.* 啤酒

Look at the picture for question 10.

10. (**A**)　The movie will start in ten minutes.　When will the
　　　movie start?
　　　A. 8:50.　　　　　B. 9:30.
　　　C. 10:10.
　　　* in（ɪn）*prep.* 再過～

第二部份

11. (**C**)　What did you do to my plants?　They are all dead now.
　　　A. Wow!　They are beautiful.
　　　B. Really?　Good for you!
　　　C. Oh, I forgot to water them.
　　　* plant（plænt）*n.* 植物　　dead（dɛd）*adj.* 死的
　　　　Good for you!　做得好!　　water（'wɔtɚ）*v.* 澆水

12. (**B**) May I borrow your ruler, please?
    A. Sure. What do you need?
    B. Sure. Here you are.
    C. Sure. I give up.

    * borrow〔'bɑro〕*v.* 借（入）   ruler〔'rulɚ〕*n.* 尺
    Here you are. 拿去吧。   ***give up*** 放棄

13. (**A**) Where were you born?
    A. I was born in Taipei.
    B. I was born in winter.
    C. I was born in November.

14. (**C**) Look! My new sneakers! My mom bought them for
    me yesterday.
    A. You had better wear your coat.
    B. What a beautiful sweater!
    C. Wow! They are really cool.

    * sneakers〔'snikɚz〕*n. pl.* 球鞋
    sweater〔'swɛtɚ〕*n.* 毛衣
    cool〔kul〕*adj.* 很酷的；很棒的

15. (**C**) What's your favorite sport?
    A. I enjoy watching TV.
    B. I like to listen to popular music.
    C. I love basketball.

    * favorite〔'fevərɪt〕*adj.* 最喜歡的
    popular music 流行音樂（= *pop music*）
    basketball〔'bæskɪt,bɔl〕*n.* 籃球

16. (**B**) It's eleven ten now, but Tom's watch is fast by five
minutes. What time does Tom's watch show now?
A. 11:30.
B. 11:15.
C. 11:10.

* *by* 表「差距」。　　show〔ʃo〕*v.* 顯示

17. (**A**) Lucy can't see the words on the blackboard clearly.
What should she wear?
A. She should wear a pair of glasses.
B. She should wear a watch.
C. She should wear a hat.

* blackboard〔'blæk,bord〕*n.* 黑板
clearly〔'klɪrlɪ〕*adv.* 清楚地
a pair of glasses 一副眼鏡

18. (**B**) Good-bye, Billy. Have a nice weekend.
A. See you later.
B. See you on Monday.
C. Wait and see.

* weekend〔'wik'ɛnd〕*n.* 週末　　*See you later.* 待會兒見。
Wait and see. 走著瞧。

19. (**A**) Who do you go to if you feel sick?
A. The doctor.
B. The mailman.
C. The neighbor.

* mailman〔'mel,mæn〕*n.* 郵差
neighbor〔'nebɚ〕*n.* 鄰居

20. (**B**) How were your tests today?

    A. I was lucky to catch them.

    B. They were easy. I think I passed them all.

    C. All of us had a good time today.

    * lucky ('lʌkɪ) *adj.* 幸運的   catch (kætʃ) *v.* 抓住;趕上

    pass (pæs) *v.* 通過;及格

    have a good time 玩得愉快

第三部份

21. (**A**) W: May I take a look at the puppy?

    M: Sure. Come closer so that you can see it more clearly.

    Question: What does the man want the woman to do?

    A. Come near him.

    B. Take away the puppy.

    C. Buy the puppy.

    * *take a look at* 看一看

    puppy ('pʌpɪ) *n.* 小狗   *take away* 拿走

22. (**B**) W: Do you mind if I close the window? It's a little cold.

    M: Not at all. In fact, I feel a bit chilly, too.

    Question: What does the man mean?

    A. He thinks he has a cold.

    B. He also thinks it is better to close the window.

    C. He doesn't want the woman to close the window.

    * cold (kold) *adj.* 冷的 *n.* 感冒   *not at all* 一點也不

    a bit 有一點 (= *a little*)   chilly ('tʃɪlɪ) *adj.* 冷的

23. (**B**) W：Where have you been? Your father and I were
　　　　　　worried to death.
　　　　M：I'm sorry. I went to Jim's house and played video
　　　　　　games with him. I know I should have called but
　　　　　　I forgot.

　　　　Question：What's the most possible relationship
　　　　　　　　　　between the two speakers?
　　　　A. Wife and husband.
　　　　B. Mother and son.
　　　　C. Sister and brother.

　　　　* worried〔'wɜɪd〕*adj.* 擔心的
　　　　　　be worried to death 擔心得要死
　　　　　　relationship〔rɪ'leʃənˌʃɪp〕*n.* 關係
　　　　　　wife〔waɪf〕*n.* 妻子
　　　　　　husband〔'hʌzbənd〕*n.* 丈夫

24. (**C**) M：This cake looks great. Mmm…., it's delicious.
　　　　　　Don't you want some?
　　　　W：No, thanks. I'm on a diet.
　　　　M：Come on, you are not fat at all.

　　　　Question：What is the woman afraid of？
　　　　A. She is afraid of the cake.
　　　　B. She is afraid of getting lost.
　　　　C. She is afraid of gaining weight.

　　　　* *be on a diet* 節食　　*come on* 拜託；少來了
　　　　　　not~at all 一點也不~　　fat〔fæt〕*adj.* 胖的
　　　　　　be afraid of 害怕　　*get lost* 迷路
　　　　　　gain weight 增加體重；變胖

25. (**B**) M：Excuse me, ma'am.　Could you tell me where the
　　　　　　 King Theater is?

　　　　　 W：I wish I could, but I am a stranger here myself.

　　　　　 M：That's all right.　Thank you, anyway.

　　　　　 Question：What does the woman mean?

　　　　　 A.　She doesn't know the man.

　　　　　 B.　She doesn't know where the theater is, either.

　　　　　 C.　She doesn't want to tell him where the theater is.

　　　　　 * ma'am〔mæm〕*n.* 太太；小姐　　theater〔'θiətə〕*n.* 戲院
　　　　　　 stranger〔'strendʒə〕*n.* 陌生人；初到 (某處) 的人
　　　　　　 That's all right. 沒關係。
　　　　　　 anyway〔'ɛnɪ,we〕*adv.* 無論如何

26. (**A**) W：Look at the window.　It's so dirty.　You should
　　　　　　 wash it more often.

　　　　　 M：I know and I will, if I have time.

　　　　　 Question：What does the man mean?

　　　　　 A.　He is too busy to wash the window.

　　　　　 B.　The window is too dirty to be washed clean.

　　　　　 C.　The window should be cleaned once a week.

　　　　　 * dirty〔'dɝtɪ〕*adj.* 骯髒的　　***too…to*～** 太…以致於不～
　　　　　　 once〔wʌns〕*adv.* 一次

27. (**C**) W：I am going to the post office to pick up my mail.
　　　　　　 Do you need anything?

　　　　　 M：Yes, please buy some five-dollar stamps for me.
　　　　　　 I've got several letters to send.

　　　　　 W：O.K.　No problem.

　　　　　 M：Thank you very much.

Question： Why is the woman going to the post office?

A. To send some letters.

B. To buy some stamps.

C. To collect her mail.

* ***pick up*** 領取（ = *collect* ）　　mail〔 mel 〕*n.* 郵件

stamp〔 stæmp 〕*n.* 郵票　　***have got*** 有（ = *have* ）

send〔 sɛnd 〕*v.* 寄（信）

28. (**B**) W： What did you think of that movie on TV last night,
Ted?

M： I was so tired that I fell asleep. I missed a large
part of it.

W： What a pity! I thought it was a great movie.

Question： According to Ted, how was the film?

A. He thinks it's a great one.

B. He was sleeping and didn't finish watching the movie.

C. He doesn't think it's good.

* ***What do you think of***～? 你認為～如何？

fall asleep 睡著　　miss〔 mɪs 〕*v.* 錯過

part〔 part 〕*n.* 部份　　***What a pity***! 真可惜！

according to 根據　　film〔 fɪlm 〕*n.* 電影（ = *movie* ）

finish〔ˈfɪnɪʃ〕*v.* 完成；看完

29. (**A**) W：What do you usually have for breakfast?

M：I usually go to McDonald's and have a Big Mac, an order of large French fries, an apple pie and hot coffee.

W：What a big appetite you have!

Question：What does the woman mean?

A. He eats a lot.

B. He eats a little.

C. He eats little.

* **Big Mac** 麥香堡   order〔'ɔrdɚ〕n.（食物的）一份
French fries 薯條   **apple pie** 蘋果派
appetite〔'æpə,taɪt〕n. 食慾；胃口
a little 一點點   little〔'lɪtḷ〕n. 很少

30. (**C**) W：What are you writing, Tom?

M：I'm writing a letter to my new pen pal introducing myself.

W：Let me see. Oh, dear! I can't understand it at all. I think you'd better type your letter.

Question：What does the woman imply?

A. Tom should buy a new typewriter.

B. Tom shouldn't write to a pen pal.

C. Tom has poor handwriting.

* **pen pal** 筆友   introduce〔,ɪntrə'djus〕v. 介紹
Oh, dear! 噢，天啊！   type〔taɪp〕v. 打字
imply〔ɪm'plaɪ〕v. 暗示
typewriter〔'taɪp,raɪtɚ〕n. 打字機
write to sb. 寫信給某人   poor〔pur〕adj. 差的
handwriting〔'hænd,raɪtɪŋ〕n. 字跡；筆跡

全民英語能力分級檢定測驗
初級聽力測驗⑤

　　本測驗分三部份，全爲三選一之選擇題，每部份各 10 題，共 30 題，作答時間約 20 分鐘。

第一部份：　看圖辨義

　　　　　　本部份共 10 題，試題冊上每題有一個圖片，請聽錄音機播出一個相關的問題，與 A、B、C 三個英語敘述後，選一個與所看到圖片最相符的答案，並在答案紙上相對的圓圈內塗黑作答。每題播出一遍，問題及選項均不印在試題冊上。

例：（看）

NT$80　　**NT$50**

（聽）

Look at the picture.　How much is the hamburger?

　　A.　It's eighty dollars.
　　B.　It's fifty-five dollars.
　　C.　It's eighteen dollars.

正確答案爲 A

Question 1

Question 2

Question 3

Question 4

Question 5

Question 6

請翻頁 ⫸

Question 7

Question 8

Question 9

Question 10

請 翻 頁 ▯⇒

第二部份： 問答

　　　　本部份共 10 題，每題錄音機會播出一個問句或直述句，
　　　　每題播出一次，聽後請從試題冊上 A、B、C 三個選項中，
　　　　選出一個最適合的回答或回應，並在答案紙上塗黑作答。

　　例：

　　（聽） Good morning, Kevin. How are you?

　　（看） A. I'm fine, thank you.
　　　　　 B. I'm in the living room.
　　　　　 C. My name is Kevin.

　　　　正確答案為 A

11. A. Yes, I did.
    B. I ate breakfast at home.
    C. At eight.

12. A. I sometimes work
       on Sunday.
    B. Sometimes I go by
       bus, and sometimes
       by bicycle.
    C. I never ride my
       bicycle to work.

13. A. I have everything
       we'll need for fishing.
    B. Where are the worms?
    C. I'm sorry. I have an
       English test tomorrow.

14. A. So do I.
    B. Neither do I.
    C. Do you like watching
       movies?

15. A. No, I wasn't. I had
　　 a cold.
　　B. No, I didn't want to
　　 come. I had a cold.
　　C. No, I didn't. I had
　　 a cold.

16. A. Sure, here are you.
　　B. Sure, here you are.
　　C. Of course, here is it.

17. A. We will pay for that.
　　B. You look great.
　　C. How nice it is! Will
　　 you come with us?

18. A. No, I told you nothing.
　　B. Thank you, too.
　　C. You are welcome.

19. A. No, I have only two
　　 hands.
　　B. Which one do you
　　 want?
　　C. Sure.

20. A. What's the matter?
　　B. That's your problem.
　　C. Why do you come
　　 to me?

請 翻 頁 ◗⟹

第三部份： 簡短對話

本部份共 10 題，每題錄音機會播出一段對話及一個相關的問題，每題播出兩次，聽後請從試題冊上 A、B、C 三個選項中，選出一個最適合的回答，並在答案紙上塗黑作答。

例：

(聽) (Woman) Good afternoon, ...Mr. Davis?

(Man) Yes.   I have an appointment with Dr. Sanders at two o'clock.   My son Tommy has a fever.

(Woman) Oh, that's too bad.   Well, please have a seat, Mr. Davis.   Dr. Sanders will be right with you.

Question: Where did this conversation take place?

(看) A.   In a post office.

B.   In a restaurant.

C.   In a doctor's office.

正確答案為 C

21. A. He is a student.
    B. He is a doctor.
    C. He is an English
       teacher.

22. A. A TV program.
    B. A birthday party.
    C. A movie.

23. A. At a restaurant.
    B. At a store.
    C. At an airport.

24. A. The man does.
    B. The woman does.
    C. Both the man and
       the woman do.

25. A. She did very well
       on the test.
    B. She didn't do very
       well on the test.
    C. The thing she did
       surprised the man.

26. A. They are going to a
       basketball game together.
    B. They are going to invite
       John to a party.
    C. They are going to the
       movies.

27. A. A hospital.
    B. A theater.
    C. A station.

28. A. She doesn't feel very well.
    B. She feels sorry.
    C. She is very excited.

29. A. Tomorrow morning.
    B. This afternoon.
    C. Tomorrow afternoon.

30. A. She doesn't want the
       man to smoke in front
       of her.
    B. She wants to smoke, too.
    C. She doesn't mind if
       the man smokes.

初級聽力測驗詳解⑤

第一部份

Look at the picture for question 1.

1. (**C**) What did the boy leave on the bus?
   A. He left a package on the bus.
   B. He left a wallet on the bus.
   C. He left an umbrella on the bus.

   * leave (liv) v. 遺留　　package ('pækɪdʒ) n. 包裹
   wallet ('wɑlɪt) n. 皮夾　　umbrella (ʌm'brɛlə) n. 雨傘

Look at the picture for question 2.

2. (**A**) What will happen to the boy?
   A. He may fall into a hole.
   B. He may hit a car.
   C. He may be stopped by an officer.

   * **happen to** 發生　　fall (fɔl) v. 掉落
   hole (hol) n. 洞　　hit (hɪt) v. 撞上
   stop (stɑp) v. 攔下來　　officer ('ɔfəsɚ) n. 警官

Look at the picture for question 3.

3. (**C**) What is the man doing?
   A. He is reading a comic book.
   B. He is watching TV.
   C. He is painting in water colors.

   * **comic book** 漫畫書　　paint (pent) v. 繪畫
   water colors 水彩

Look at the picture for question 4.

4. (**A**) Which of the following statements is correct?

    A. Tom is shorter than John.

    B. Bill is shorter than Tom.

    C. John is the tallest of the three.

    * following ('faləwɪŋ) adj. 下列的

      statement ('stetmənt) n. 敘述

      correct (kə'rɛkt) adj. 正確的

      short (ʃɔrt) adj. 矮的

Look at the picture for question 5.

5. (**C**) What is the man on the roof doing?

    A. He is running after a thief.

    B. He is blowing his whistle.

    C. He is trying to escape.

    * roof (ruf) n. 屋頂　　*run after* 追

      thief (θif) n. 小偷　　whistle ('hwɪsl̩) n. 哨子

      blow one's whistle 吹哨子

      escape (ə'skep) v. 逃走

Look at the picture for question 6.

6. (**A**) What is Tom doing?

    A. He is watching TV.

    B. He is having dinner.

    C. He is exercising.

    * have (hæv) v. 吃　　exercise ('ɛksə‚saɪz) v. 運動

Look at the picture for question 7.

7. (**B**) Which statement is correct?

    A. Mary is sick and is lying on the bed.

    B. Mary brings some flowers to Helen.

    C. Helen buys some flowers for Mary.

    * statement〔'stetmənt〕*n.* 敘述

      correct〔kə'rɛkt〕*adj.* 正確的   lie〔laɪ〕*v.* 躺

      visit〔'vɪzɪt〕*v.* 探望   ***buy* sth. *for* sb.** 買某物給某人

Look at the picture for question 8.

8. (**B**) Why is the man so afraid?

    A. He fears the lion will come out of the cage.

    B. He is afraid because the lion may eat him.

    C. He sees the lion running after him.

    * afraid〔ə'fred〕*adj.* 害怕的   fear〔fɪr〕*v.* 害怕

      lion〔'laɪən〕*n.* 獅子   cage〔kedʒ〕*n.* 籠子

Look at the picture for question 9.

9. (**C**) What is the boy doing?

    A. He is seeing a doctor.

    B. He is jogging.

    C. He is studying.

Look at the picture for question 10.

10. (**A**) Paul is sorry for being twenty-five minutes late. What time does his class begin?

    A. 8:15.

    B. 9:05.

    C. 8:40.

    * late〔let〕*adj.* 遲到的

第二部份

11. (**C**)　What time did you eat breakfast this morning?
　　　A.　Yes, I did.
　　　B.　I ate breakfast at home.
　　　C.　At eight.

12. (**B**)　How do you go to work?
　　　A.　I sometimes work on Sunday.
　　　B.　Sometimes I go by bus, and sometimes by bicycle.
　　　C.　I never ride my bicycle to work.

13. (**C**)　Let's go fishing, shall we?
　　　A.　I have everything we'll need for fishing.
　　　B.　Where are the worms?
　　　C.　I'm sorry.　I have an English test tomorrow.
　　　* ***go fishing*** 去釣魚　　　worm〔wɝm〕*n.* 蟲

14. (**A**)　I like playing computer games more than watching movies.
　　　A.　So do I.
　　　B.　Neither do I.
　　　C.　Do you like watching movies?
　　　* computer〔kəmˈpjutɚ〕*n.* 電腦
　　　like A ***more than*** B　喜歡 A 甚於 B
　　　watch movies 看電影（ = *see movies* ）
　　　So do I. 我也是。　　***Neither do I.*** 我也不（喜歡）。

15. (**A**) Were you in school yesterday?
   A. No, I wasn't. I had a cold.
   B. No, I didn't want to come. I had a cold.
   C. No, I didn't. I had a cold.

   * **in school** 上學中 (= *at school*)
   have a cold 感冒 (= *catch a cold*)

16. (**B**) Could you pass me the dictionary, please?
   A. Sure, here are you.
   B. Sure, here you are.
   C. Of course, here is it.

   * pass (pæs) *v.* 傳遞 dictionary ('dɪkʃən,ɛrɪ) *n.* 字典
   Here you are. 你要的東西在這裡；拿去吧。(= *Here it is.*)

17. (**C**) Everything in the store is on sale today.
   A. We will pay for that.
   B. You look great.
   C. How nice it is! Will you come with us?

   * **on sale** 大拍賣 **pay for** 付～的錢

18. (**C**) Thank you for telling us the news.
   A. No, I told you nothing.
   B. Thank you, too.
   C. You are welcome.

   * news (njuz) *n.* 消息

19. (**C**) I can't do this myself. Would you please give me a hand?
   A. No, I have only two hands.
   B. Which one do you want?
   C. Sure.

   * **give** *sb.* **a hand** 幫忙某人 (= *do sb. a favor* = *help sb.*)

20. (**A**) I'm not feeling very well, Doctor.

    A. What's the matter?

    B. That's your problem.

    C. Why do you come to me?

    * ***What's the matter?*** 怎麼了？（ = *What's wrong?*）

第三部份

21. (**C**) M：Are you a teacher?

    W：No, I'm a student. And what do you do?

    M：I'm an English teacher.

    Question：What does the man do?

    A. He is a student.

    B. He is a doctor.

    C. He is an English teacher.

    * ***What do you do?*** 你從事什麼行業？（ = *What are you?*）

22. (**B**) M：Tomorrow is my birthday and we are going to have a party. Would you like to come?

    W：Sure, what time will the party begin?

    M：It will begin at seven-thirty.

    Question：What are the man and woman talking about?

    A. A TV program.

    B. A birthday party.

    C. A movie.

    * ***talk about*** 談論　　program〔'progræm〕*n.* 節目

23. (**B**) W：Can I help you?

　　　　M：Yes, what's on sale today?

　　　　W：Everything.　Today is our grand opening.

　　　Question：Where does this conversation take place?

　　　A. At a restaurant.

　　　B. At a store.

　　　C. At an airport.

　　　* grand〔grænd〕*adj.* 盛大的　　opening〔'opənɪŋ〕*n.* 開幕
　　　　conversation〔,kɑnvɚ'seʃən〕*n.* 對話
　　　　take place 發生　　airport〔'ɛr,port〕*n.* 機場

24. (**B**) M：You speak very good English.

　　　　W：Thank you.

　　　　M：How long have you studied English?

　　　　W：I have studied English for three years.

　　　Question：Who speaks very good English?

　　　A. The man does.

　　　B. The woman does.

　　　C. Both the man and the woman do.

25. (**B**) M：You don't look very good.　Are you all right?

　　　　W：No, I'm not.　That test was really hard.　I didn't
　　　　　　do very well.

　　　　M：That doesn't surprise me.

　　　　W：Why not?　We studied together all evening.

　　　Question：How did the woman do on the test?

　　　A. She did very well on the test.

　　　B. She didn't do very well on the test.

　　　C. The thing she did surprised the man.

　　　* ***do well***　（考試）考得好　　surprise〔sə'praɪz〕*v.* 使驚訝

26. (**A**) M：I'm going to go to a basketball game. I have three tickets. Can you go?

W：Of course. Who will use the third ticket?

M：I'm going to ask John. He likes basketball.

Question：What are the man and woman going to do?

A. They are going to a basketball game together.

B. They are going to invite John to a party.

C. They are going to the movies.

* invite〔ɪn'vaɪt〕*v.* 邀請
  go to the movies 去看電影

27. (**C**) M：What's the rush?

W：I have to catch a train.

M：Why do you have to?

W：That's the last train tonight.

Question：Where is the woman going?

A. A hospital.

B. A theater.

C. A station.

* rush〔rʌʃ〕*n.* 匆忙
  What's the rush? 你在急什麼？
  catch〔kætʃ〕*v.* 趕上（車）
  hospital〔'hɑspɪtl̩〕*n.* 醫院　　theater〔'θiətɚ〕*n.* 戲院
  station〔'steʃən〕*n.* 車站

28. (**A**)　M：How do you feel today?
　　　　　W：I don't feel very well.
　　　　　M：I am sorry to hear that.　Did you see the doctor?
　　　　　W：Yes, I did.

　　　　Question：How does the woman feel?
　　　　A. She doesn't feel very well.
　　　　B. She feels sorry.
　　　　C. She is very excited.

　　　* sorry ('sɔrɪ) adj. 遺憾的；難過的
　　　　excited (ɪk'saɪtɪd) adj. 興奮的

29. (**C**)　M：We are free all afternoon tomorrow.
　　　　　W：What do you have in mind?
　　　　　M：I plan to go hiking.

　　　　Question：When will the man go hiking?
　　　　A. Tomorrow morning.
　　　　B. This afternoon.
　　　　C. Tomorrow afternoon.

　　　* free (fri) adj. 有空的
　　　　have sth. in mind 在想某事；在計劃某事
　　　　hike (haɪk) v. 健行；徒步旅行

30. (**A**)　M：Would you mind if I smoke?
　　　　　W：I sure would.
　　　　　M：Sorry, I'll go away.

　　　　Question：What does the woman mean?
　　　　A. She doesn't want the man to smoke in front of her.
　　　　B. She wants to smoke, too.
　　　　C. She doesn't mind if the man smokes.

　　　* mind (maɪnd) v. 介意　　smoke (smok) v. 抽煙
　　　　sure (ʃur) adv. 當然　　*in front of* 在～面前

全民英語能力分級檢定測驗
初級聽力測驗⑥

本測驗分三部份，全為三選一之選擇題，每部份各 10 題，共 30 題，作答時間約 20 分鐘。

第一部份： 看圖辨義

本部份共 10 題，試題冊上每題有一個圖片，請聽錄音機播出一個相關的問題，與 A、B、C 三個英語敘述後，選一個與所看到圖片最相符的答案，並在答案紙上相對的圓圈內塗黑作答。每題播出一遍，問題及選項均不印在試題冊上。

例：（看）

（聽）

Look at the picture. How much is the hamburger?

    A. It's eighty dollars.
    B. It's fifty-five dollars.
    C. It's eighteen dollars.

正確答案為 A

Question 1

Question 2

Question 3

Question 4

$550 $690

Question 5

To \ Train	1314	520	168
Taipei	07:40	08:25	09:10
Taichung	09:55	10:18	11:20
Kaohsiung	12:16	14:03	13:30

Question 6

請翻頁 ◗◗⟹

Question 7

Name	Stanley	Sandra	Steven
Birth Date	Aug. 15th, 1995	Oct. 11th, 1997	Sept. 2nd, 1999
Birth Place	Taipei	New York	London

Question 8

Grandpa　Kevin　Dad　Mom　Sister

Question 9

	Taipei	Tokyo	Sydney
Spring	Warm and wet	Cool and wet	Warm and dry
Summer	Hot and wet	Hot and dry	Cool and dry
Fall	Hot and dry	Warm and dry	Warm and dry
Winter	Cool and dry	Cold and dry	Hot and wet

Question 10

請 翻 頁 ▯⟹

第二部份：問答

本部份共 10 題，每題錄音機會播出一個問句或直述句，
每題播出一次，聽後請從試題冊上 A、B、C 三個選項中
選出一個最適合的回答或回應，並在答案紙上塗黑作答

例：

（聽）　Good morning, Kevin. How are you?

（看）　A. I'm fine, thank you.
　　　　B. I'm in the living room.
　　　　C. My name is Kevin.

正確答案為 A

11. A. That's my sister,
　　　　Sherry.

　　B. That's my brother,
　　　　Stanley.

　　C. Stella is my sister.

12. A. $25,000,000.

　　B. $2,500,000.

　　C. $250,000.

13. A. It was your fault,
　　　　wasn't it?

　　B. Did you get hurt?

　　C. That's terrible! Was
　　　　anyone hurt?

14. A. It is made in U.S.A.

　　B. It is in the closet over
　　　　there.

　　C. It is a white dress.

15. A. Yes, I am. I'm an
       American.
    B. No, I don't.
    C. No, never. Have you?

16. A. I'm sorry to hear this.
    B. Excuse me.
    C. Congratulations!

17. A. Yes, the right number
       is 2371-5620.
    B. Sorry, it's 2374-5620.
    C. This is she speaking.

18. A. My name is Daisy.
    B. I am a worker.
    C. It's mine.

19. A. How about some
       bread?
    B. How about a sweater?
    C. How about a walk?

20. A. Too bad!
    B. Had a good time!
    C. Bring some T-shirts!

請 翻 頁 ◖⟹

第三部份： 簡短對話

本部份共 10 題，每題錄音機會播出一段對話及一個相關的問題，每題播出兩次，聽後請從試題冊上 A、B、C 三個選項中，選出一個最適合的回答，並在答案紙上塗黑作答。

例：

(聽)　(Woman)　Good afternoon, ...Mr. Davis?

　　　　(Man)　　Yes.　I have an appointment with Dr. Sanders at two o'clock.　My son Tommy has a fever.

　　　　(Woman)　Oh, that's too bad.　Well, please have a seat, Mr. Davis.　Dr. Sanders will be right with you.

　　　　Question:　Where did this conversation take place?

(看)　A.　In a post office.

　　　　B.　In a restaurant.

　　　　C.　In a doctor's office.

正確答案為 C

21. A. In a fast-food
       restaurant.
    B. In a post office.
    C. In a bookstore.

22. A. She is buying a table.
    B. She is eating.
    C. She is reserving a
       table.

23. A. 10 hours.
    B. 6 hours.
    C. 4 hours.

24. A. He broke his bicycle.
    B. He turned right and
       went to school.
    C. He had a bad day.

25. A. By taxi.
    B. By bus.
    C. On foot.

26. A. Wash dishes.
    B. Buy the dishwashing
       soap.
    C. Turn on the cupboard.

27. A. Husband and wife.
    B. Father and daughter.
    C. Customer and clerk.

28. A. In a bank.
    B. In a post office.
    C. In a pharmacy.

29. A. To drink much water
       and stay in bed.
    B. An eye examination.
    C. A place to sit and rest.

30. A. A grocery list.
    B. Salt and sugar.
    C. A jar of jam.

初級聽力測驗詳解⑥

第一部份

Look at the picture for question 1.

1. (**B**) What's Willy talking about?
    A. The food he likes.
    B. The sports he likes.
    C. The movie star he likes.
    * ***talk about*** 談論   star〔stɑr〕*n.* 明星

Look at the picture for question 2.

2. (**B**) Who's the girl John wants to invite to his birthday party?
    A. Jane.
    B. Linda.
    C. Helen.
    * invite〔ɪn'vaɪt〕*v.* 邀請

Look at the picture for question 3.

3. (**C**) Which subject is the most difficult?
    A. Chinese.
    B. English.
    C. Math.
    * subject〔'sʌbdʒɪkt〕*n.* 科目
    difficult〔'dɪfə,kʌlt〕*adj.* 困難的   math〔mæθ〕*n.* 數學

Look at the picture for question 4.

4. (**C**) Roger bought Barbara a hat and a watch. How much did he spend?
    A. $550.   B. $690.
    C. $1240.

Look at the picture for question 5.

5. (**B**) Charles took a train from Taichung and he arrived
at Kaohsiung at 14:03. When did Charles board
the train?
A. At 9:55.
B. At 10:18.
C. At 11:20.
* arrive〔ə'raɪv〕v. 到達　　board〔bord〕v. 上（車）

Look at the picture for question 6.

6. (**A**) Where's the pen?
A. Under the desk.
B. On the desk.
C. A book and a picture.

Look at the picture for question 7.

7. (**B**) Where was Sandra born?
A. On Oct. 11, 1997.
B. In New York.
C. In September.

Look at the picture for question 8.

8. (**C**) Who is the man wearing glasses and a hat?
A. Kevin.
B. Kevin's father.
C. Kevin's grandfather.
* grandfather〔'grænd,faðɚ〕n. 祖父（= grandpa〔'grændpɑ〕）

Look at the picture for question 9.

9. (**B**) What's the spring weather like in Tokyo?
  A. Warm and wet.
  B. Cool and wet.
  C. Warm and dry.

  * spring〔sprɪŋ〕*n.* 春天　　weather〔'wɛðɚ〕*n.* 天氣
    Tokyo〔'tokɪ,o〕*n.* 東京　　warm〔wɔrm〕*adj.* 溫暖的
    wet〔wɛt〕*adj.* 潮濕的　　cool〔kul〕*adj.* 涼爽的
    dry〔draɪ〕*adj.* 乾燥的

Look at the picture for question 10.

10. (**B**) How did Jack feel about the movie?
  A. They were at the movie theater.
  B. Jack felt bored.
  C. Rose felt impressed.

  * theater〔'θiətɚ〕*n.* 戲院　　bored〔bord〕*adj.* 無聊的
    impressed〔ɪm'prɛst〕*adj.* 印象深刻的；感動的

第二部份

11. (**B**) Who is the thin boy standing over there, Stella?
  A. That's my sister, Sherry.
  B. That's my brother, Stanley.
  C. Stella is my sister.

  * thin〔θɪn〕*adj.* 瘦的

12. (**B**) Mr. Collins bought a new apartment for $2,500,000.
  How much did Mr. Collins spend?
  A. $25,000,000.
  B. $2,500,000.
  C. $250,000.

  * apartment〔ə'pɑrtmənt〕*n.* 公寓

13. (**C**) This morning I saw a motorcylist run into a bus near my school.
    A. It was your fault, wasn't it?
    B. Did you get hurt?
    C. That's terrible! Was anyone hurt?

    * motorcyclist ('motə،saɪklɪst) *n.* 機車騎士
      run into 撞到　　fault (fɔlt) *n.* 過錯
      hurt (hɜt) *v.* 傷害　　***get hurt*** 受傷
      terrible ('tɛrəbḷ) *adj.* 可怕的；糟糕的

14. (**B**) Where is the white dress I bought you last week?
    A. It is made in U.S.A.
    B. It is in the closet over there.
    C. It is a white dress.

    * dress (drɛs) *n.* 洋裝　　closet ('klɑzɪt) *n.* 衣櫥

15. (**C**) Have you ever been to New York?
    A. Yes, I am. I'm an American.
    B. No, I don't.
    C. No, never. Have you?

    * ***have been to*** 曾經去過

16. (**A**) Dr. Wang told Mrs. Lee that her husband got cancer from smoking.
    A. I'm sorry to hear this.
    B. Excuse me.
    C. Congratulations!

    * cancer ('kænsə) *n.* 癌症　　smoke (smok) *v.* 抽煙
      congratulations (kən،grætʃə'leʃənz) *n. pl.* 恭喜

17. (**B**) Is this 2371-5520?
    A. Yes, the right number is 2371-5620.
    B. Sorry, it's 2374-5620.
    C. This is she speaking.

    * right ﹝ raɪt ﹞ *adj.* 正確的
    This is she speaking. (電話中) 我就是。

18. (**A**) Hello, my name is Alex. What's yours?
    A. My name is Daisy.
    B. I am a worker.
    C. It's mine.

19. (**A**) Mom, I've just finished cleaning my room. Now I am very hungry.
    A. How about some bread?
    B. How about a sweater?
    C. How about a walk?

    * finish ﹝'fɪnɪʃ ﹞ *v.* 完成   clean ﹝ klin ﹞ *v.* 打掃
    hungry ﹝'hʌŋgrɪ ﹞ *adj.* 飢餓的
    How about~? ~如何?   bread ﹝ brɛd ﹞ *n.* 麵包
    sweater ﹝'swɛtɚ﹞ *n.* 毛衣   walk ﹝ wɔk ﹞ *n.* 散步

20. (**C**) Our family will take a trip to Singapore during the Chinese New Year.
    A. Too bad!
    B. Had a good time! (應改成 *Have a good time!*)
    C. Bring some T-shirts!

    * *take a trip* 去旅行   *Too bad!* 真糟糕!;太可惜了!
    have a good time 玩得愉快   T-shirt ﹝'ti,ʃɜt ﹞ *n.* T 恤

第三部份

21. (**A**) M : May I help you?

W : Yes, 3 hamburgers and 2 large fries, please.

M : Anything to drink?

W : 2 large cokes.

M : To go or for here?

W : To go.

Question : Where is the woman?

A. In a fast-food restaurant.

B. In a post office.

C. In a bookstore.

* fries〔fraɪz〕*n. pl.* 薯條（= *French fries*）
  to go（食物）外帶　　*for here* 內用；這裏吃
  fast-food〔'fæst'fud〕*adj.* 專賣速食的
  post office 郵局　　bookstore〔'buk,stor〕*n.* 書店

22. (**C**) M : Hello, this is Henry's Restaurant.

W : I want to reserve a table for four.

M : Your name, please.

W : Annie Brown.

Question : What is the woman doing?

A. She is buying a table.

B. She is eating.

C. She is reserving a table.

* reserve〔rɪ'zɝv〕*v.* 預訂

23. (**A**)　W：Where did you go last night, Frank?

M：I went to Kenting to see shooting stars with Peter.

W：How did you get to Kenting?

M：I spent six hours driving to Kaohsiung and then Peter spent four hours driving to Kenting. There were so many cars on the road.

Question：How many hours did Frank and Peter spend getting to Kenting?

A. 10 hours.

B. 6 hours.

C. 4 hours.

* ***Kenting*** 墾丁　　***shooting star*** 流星

24. (**C**)　W：Why were you late for school today?

M：My bicycle was broken and I waited for the bus for a long time.

W：Today was not your day. Nothing seemed to go right.

Question：What happened to the boy?

A. He broke his bicycle.

B. He turned right and went to school.

C. He had a bad day.

* late〔let〕*adj.* 遲到的

broken〔'brokən〕*adj.* 故障的

Today was not your day. 今天你運氣不好。

seem〔sim〕*v.* 似乎　　***go right*** 順利

break〔brek〕*v.* 打破；弄壞

turn right 右轉　　***have a bad day***（某日）過得不順利

25. (**C**) W：When will the next bus come?

M：Maybe in another forty minutes.

W：Another 40 minutes! Oh, how about walking home then?

M：It seems we have no other choice.

Question：How will the speakers go home?

A. By taxi.

B. By bus.

C. On foot.

* ***in another forty minutes*** 再過四十分鐘

How about~? ~如何? then〔ðɛn〕*adv.* 那麼

choice〔tʃɔɪs〕*n.* 選擇 ***on foot*** 步行

26. (**A**) W：It's your turn to do the dishes, Larry.

M：Yes, mom. Where is the dishwashing soap?

W：Beneath the sink.

M：Where do the dishes go?

W：On the top shelf of the cupboard.

Question：What does Larry's mom want him to do?

A. Wash dishes.

B. Buy the dishwashing soap.

C. Turn on the cupboard.

* turn〔tɝn〕*n.* 輪流 ***It's one's turn to V.*** 輪到某人~

do the dishes 洗碗 ***dishwashing soap*** 洗碗精

beneath〔bɪ'niθ〕*prep.* 在~下面

sink〔sɪŋk〕*n.* (廚房) 水槽;洗手台

Where do the dishes go? 碗盤要放哪裏?

top〔tɑp〕*adj.* 最上層的;最高的 shelf〔ʃɛlf〕*n.* 架子

cupboard〔'kʌbɚd〕*n.* 碗櫥 ***turn on*** 打開 (電源)

27. (**C**)　M：One ticket to Los Angeles.

　　　　　W：Round trip or one way?

　　　　　M：Round trip, please.

　　　　　W：It's 758 dollars.　Cash or charge?

　　　　　M：Cash.　Where do I go?

　　　　　W：Gate 15.　Have a nice trip.

　　　　　M：Thank you.

　　　　Question：What's probably the relationship of the
　　　　　　　　　speakers?

　　　　A.　Husband and wife.

　　　　B.　Father and daughter.

　　　　C.　Customer and clerk.

　　*　*round trip*　（同路線）來回旅行

　　　　cf. *round-trip ticket* 來回票

　　　　one way 單程　　*cf.* *one-way ticket* 單程票

　　　　cash〔kæʃ〕*n.* 現金；付現

　　　　charge〔tʃɑrdʒ〕*n.* 刷卡　　gate〔get〕*n.* 登機門

　　　　Have a nice trip. 祝旅途愉快。

　　　　relationship〔rɪ'leʃənˌʃɪp〕*n.* 關係

　　　　customer〔'kʌstəmɚ〕*n.* 顧客

　　　　clerk〔klɜk〕*n.* 職員

28. (**B**)　M：I'd like to buy a money order.

　　　　　W：Fill out this form and go to Window 3.

　　　　　M：What about stamps, registered mail and surface mail?

　　　　　W：Any window but Window 3.

　　　　　M：Thank you.

Question: Where are the speakers?

A. In a bank.

B. In a post office.

C. In a pharmacy.

* ***money order*** 匯票　　***fill out*** 填寫 (= *fill in*)
　form (fɔrm) *n.* 表格　　***What about~?*** ～怎麼樣？
　stamp (stæmp) *n.* 郵票　　***registered mail*** 掛號信
　surface mail 平信　　but (bʌt) *prep.* 除了 (= *except*)
　pharmacy ('farməsɪ) *n.* 藥局

29. (**A**)　M: Hi, Debby. What seems to be the problem?

　　　W: I threw up this morning and I have a stomachache.

　　　M: I'll take a look. Have a seat.

　　　W: Thanks. And I've got a runny nose.

　　　M: You have the flu.

Question: What does Debby need?

A. To drink much water and stay in bed.

B. An eye examination.

C. A place to sit and rest.

* problem ('prabləm) *n.* 問題
　throw up 嘔吐　　stomachache ('stʌmək,ek) *n.* 胃痛
　take a look 看一看
　Have a seat. 請坐。(= *Sit down.*)
　have got 有 (= *have*)　　***runny nose*** 流鼻水
　flu (flu) *n.* 流行性感冒 (= influenza (,ɪnflu'ɛnzə))
　examination (ɪg,zæmə'neʃən) *n.* 檢查
　rest (rɛst) *v.* 休息

30. (**A**) M：I'm going grocery shopping. What do we need?

W：We're out of salt and sugar.

M：All right. And do we need soy sauce and catsup?

W：No, but we need a jar of jam.

Question：What are the speakers talking about?

A. A grocery list.

B. Salt and sugar.

C. A jar of jam.

* grocery (ˈgrosɚɪ) *n.* 雜貨店；雜貨

go grocery shopping 去雜貨店購物

be out of 用完 (= *run out of*)

salt (sɔlt) *n.* 鹽　　sugar (ˈʃʊgɚ) *n.* 糖

all right 好的　　***soy sauce*** 醬油

catsup (ˈkætsəp) *n.* 蕃茄醬 (= ketchup (ˈkɛtʃəp))

jar (dʒɑr) *n.* 罐子；廣口瓶　　jam (dʒæm) *n.* 果醬

list (lɪst) *n.* 清單

【劉毅老師的話】

這本書有些題目較實際考試難，是給你的聽力訓練，出乎其上，必得其中，出乎其中，必得其下。

全民英語能力分級檢定測驗
初級聽力測驗⑦

　　本測驗分三部份，全為三選一之選擇題，每部份各 10 題，共 30 題，作答時間約 20 分鐘。

第一部份： 看圖辨義

　　　　　本部份共 10 題，試題冊上每題有一個圖片，請聽錄音機播出一個相關的問題，與 A、B、C 三個英語敘述後，選一個與所看到圖片最相符的答案，並在答案紙上相對的圓圈內塗黑作答。每題播出一遍，問題及選項均不印在試題冊上。

例：（看）

NT$80　　NT$50

（聽）

Look at the picture.　How much is the hamburger?

　　A. It's eighty dollars.
　　B. It's fifty-five dollars.
　　C. It's eighteen dollars.

正確答案為 A

Question 1

Question 2

Question 3

Question 4

Question 5

Question 6

請 翻 頁 ⫸

Question 7

Question 8

Question 9

Question 10

Michael

請 翻 頁 ◗▢⟹

第二部份： 問答

本部份共 10 題，每題錄音機會播出一個問句或直述句，
每題播出一次，聽後請從試題冊上 A、B、C 三個選項中，
選出一個最適合的回答或回應，並在答案紙上塗黑作答。

例：

（聽） Good morning, Kevin. How are you?

（看） A.　I'm fine, thank you.
　　　 B.　I'm in the living room.
　　　 C.　My name is Kevin.

正確答案為 A

11. A. Yes, I like watermelon best.
　　B. Banana is my favorite.
　　C. Pineapples are now in season.

12. A. I'd like to have it fixed.
　　B. I've had a problem with that machine, too.
　　C. I don't know. I'm a mechanical illiterate.

13. A. Once a week.
　　B. Some other day.
　　C. Only one time.

14. A. I went to the library with Leo.
　　B. I don't know. Do you have any suggestions?
　　C. I'll call you when I get home.

15. A. What flavor do you like?
    B. I put it in the refrigerator.
    C. No, there's still a little left.

16. A. Use your own computer.
    B. I want you to do it right now.
    C. I have to send it tomorrow.

17. A. I'm from California.
    B. I live in Japan.
    C. My apartment number is 203.

18. A. Jane is.
    B. Elsa is taller than Jane.
    C. Elsa works much more carefully than Jane does.

19. A. It looks like rain.
    B. It is tasty.
    C. It tastes like strawberry.

20. A. He sold it to his neighbor.
    B. He needs money for his trip to Europe.
    C. He bought it two years ago.

請 翻 頁 Ⅱⵊ⟹

第三部份： 簡短對話

本部份共 10 題，每題錄音機會播出一段對話及一個相關
的問題，每題播出兩次，聽後請從試題冊上 A、B、C 三
個選項中，選出一個最適合的回答，並在答案紙上塗黑
作答。

例：

（聽）(Woman) Good afternoon, …Mr. Davis?

(Man) Yes. I have an appointment with Dr. Sanders at two o'clock. My son Tommy has a fever.

(Woman) Oh, that's too bad. Well, please have a seat, Mr. Davis. Dr. Sanders will be right with you.

Question: Where did this conversation take place?

（看）A. In a post office.

B. In a restaurant.

C. In a doctor's office.

正確答案為 C

21. A. She helps the patients.
    B. She sells clothes.
    C. She answers the phone.

22. A. She'll buy the bicycle.
    B. She'll take a look at
       the bicycle.
    C. She'll leave the store.

23. A. Game shows.
    B. Talk shows.
    C. Soap operas.

24. A. He has to catch a train.
    B. He needs to be home
       in time for dinner.
    C. He has to go to the bank.

25. A. Wonderfully.
    B. So-so.
    C. Terribly.

26. A. She dialed the wrong
       number.
    B. She talked to Ricky.
    C. She lied to Ricky.

27. A. They went to a great
       movie.
    B. They went shopping.
    C. They had a
       wonderful meal.

28. A. At a bookstore.
    B. At a drugstore.
    C. At a restaurant.

29. A. She's so tired that
       she'll go to the
       library.
    B. She's tired enough
       to go to the library.
    C. She's too tired to
       go to the library.

30. A. Leave a message.
    B. Go out.
    C. Talk with Mr.
       Brown.

初級聽力測驗詳解 ⑦

第一部份

Look at the picture for question 1.

1. (**A**) What is the man doing?

    A. He is playing golf.

    B. He is playing the piano.

    C. He is jumping rope.

    * golf〔gɑlf〕*n.* 高爾夫球   piano〔pɪ'æno〕*n.* 鋼琴

    rope〔rop〕*n.* 繩子   *jump rope* 跳繩

Look at the picture for question 2.

2. (**C**) What kind of store does the man own?

    A. A laundry.

    B. A department store.

    C. A grocery store.

    * kind〔kaɪnd〕*n.* 種類   own〔on〕*v.* 擁有

    laundry〔'lɔndrɪ〕*n.* 洗衣店

    grocery store 雜貨店

Look at the picture for question 3.

3. (**B**) Where can you see this?

    A. In a zoo.

    B. At a temple.

    C. At a gym.

    * temple〔'tɛmpl̩〕*n.* 寺廟   gym〔dʒɪm〕*n.* 體育館

Look at the picture for question 4.

4. (**B**) What does this place look like?
    A. It looks like a classroom at a school.
    B. It looks like an airport.
    C. It looks like a gas station.
    * airport ('ɛr,port) *n.* 機場   *gas station* 加油站

Look at the picture for question 5.

5. (**C**) What is the man holding?
    A. He's holding a spoon and a cup.
    B. He's holding a pen and a ruler.
    C. He's holding a knife and a fork.
    * hold (hold) *v.* 拿著   spoon (spun) *n.* 湯匙
    ruler ('rulɚ) *n.* 尺   knife (naɪf) *n.* 刀子
    fork (fɔrk) *n.* 叉子

Look at the picture for question 6.

6. (**A**) What happened to the man?
    A. He was bitten by a dog.
    B. He broke his leg.
    C. He was wet all over.
    * bite (baɪt) *v.* 咬（三態變化為：bite-bit-bitten）
    break (brek) *v.* 折斷   wet (wɛt) *adj.* 濕的
    all over 全身

Look at the picture for question 7.

7. (**B**) What is beside the bookbag?
    A. Some fruit.
    B. Some books.
    C. Some pens.
    * beside (bɪ'saɪd) *prep.* 在～旁邊
    bookbag ('buk,bæg) *n.* 書包

Look at the picture for question 8.

8. (**C**) What did Mike do at three o'clock today?

A. He was taking a nap.

B. He was busy talking on the phone.

C. He was in a meeting.

* nap〔næp〕*n.* 小睡　　***take a nap*** 小睡

be busy + *V-ing*　忙於~

meeting〔'mitɪŋ〕*n.* 會議

Look at the picture for question 9.

9. (**B**) What does the sign mean?

A. It means "Help Wanted."

B. It means "Danger."

C. It means "Keep Off the Grass."

* sign〔saɪn〕*n.* 告示牌　　***Help Wanted.*** 徵人。

danger〔'dendʒɚ〕*n.* 危險　　***keep off*** 遠離

grass〔græs〕*n.* 草

Keep Off the Grass. 請勿踐踏草地。

Look at the picture for question 10.

10. (**C**) What is Michael?

A. He's a driver.

B. He's a postman.

C. He's a painter.

* ***What is*** *sb.*? 某人從事什麼行業？

postman〔'postmən〕*n.* 郵差（= *mailman*）

painter〔'pentɚ〕*n.* 畫家

第二部份

11. (**B**)　What kind of fruit do you like best?

A. Yes, I like watermelon best.

B. Banana is my favorite.

C. Pineapples are now in season.

* watermelon ('wɔtɚ,mɛlən) *n.* 西瓜

banana (bə'nænə) *n.* 香蕉

favorite ('fevərɪt) *n.* 最喜愛的人或物

pineapple ('paɪn,æpl) *n.* 鳳梨　　***in season*** 正當時令

12. (**C**)　What's wrong with this machine?

A. I'd like to have it fixed.

B. I've had a problem with that machine, too.

C. I don't know. I'm a mechanical illiterate.

* ***What's wrong with***~?　~怎麼了？

machine (mə'ʃin) *n.* 機器　　fix (fɪks) *v.* 修理

have sth. fixed 修理某物

mechanical (mə'kænɪkl) *adj.* 機械的

illiterate (ɪ'lɪtərɪt) *n.* 文盲

mechanical illiterate 機械白痴；完全不懂機械的人

13. (**C**)　How many times have you been to Las Vegas?

A. Once a week.

B. Some other day.

C. Only one time.

* ***have been to*** 曾經去過

Las Vegas (lɑs'vegəs) *n.* 拉斯維加斯（位於美國內華達州
的賭城）

Some other day. 改天。

14. (**A**) Where did you go after dinner last night?

        A. I went to the library with Leo.

        B. I don't know. Do you have any suggestions?

        C. I'll call you when I get home.

        * suggestion (sə'dʒɛstʃən) *n.* 建議

15. (**C**) Did you finish all that ice cream already?

        A. What flavor do you like?

        B. I put it in the refrigerator.

        C. No, there's still a little left.

        * flavor ('flevɚ) *n.* 口味
        refrigerator (rɪ'frɪdʒə,retɚ) *n.* 冰箱
        leave (liv) *v.* 剩下

16. (**B**) Mr. Parker, when do you want me to type this letter?

        A. Use your own computer.

        B. I want you to do it right now.

        C. I have to send it tomorrow.

        * type (taɪp) *v.* 打字   ***right now*** 立刻;馬上
        send (sɛnd) *v.* 寄

17. (**A**) Which state are you from?

        A. I'm from California.

        B. I live in Japan.

        C. My apartment number is 203.

        * state (stet) *n.* 州
        California (,kælə'fɔrnɪə) *n.* 加州
        apartment (ə'pɑrtmənt) *n.* 公寓

18. (**C**) Who works more carefully, Jane or Elsa?

　　A. Jane is.

　　B. Elsa is taller than Jane.

　　C. Elsa works much more carefully than Jane does.

　　* carefully ('kɛrfəlɪ) *adv.* 小心地；仔細地

19. (**C**) What does it taste like?

　　A. It looks like rain.

　　B. It is tasty.

　　C. It tastes like strawberry.

　　* taste (test) *v.* 嚐起來

　　It looks like rain. 看起來要下雨了。

　　tasty ('testɪ) *adj.* 好吃的

　　strawberry ('strɔ,bɛrɪ) *n.* 草莓

20. (**B**) Why is Mark selling his car?

　　A. He sold it to his neighbor.

　　B. He needs money for his trip to Europe.

　　C. He bought it two years ago.

　　* neighbor ('nebɚ) *n.* 鄰居　　trip (trɪp) *n.* 旅行

　　Europe ('jurəp) *n.* 歐洲

第三部份

21. (**A**)　M：Where do you work?

W：I work in a hospital.

M：Oh, really?　And what do you do there?

W：I'm a nurse.

Question：What does the woman do?

A. She helps the patients.

B. She sells clothes.

C. She answers the phone.

* nurse〔nɝs〕*n.* 護士　　patient〔'peʃənt〕*n.* 病人

clothes〔kloz〕*n. pl.* 衣服

answer the phone 接電話

22. (**C**)　M：Good evening.

W：How much is this bicycle?

M：It's on sale.　It's only $500.

W：Five hundred dollars!　Well, I'm just looking, thanks.

Question：What will the woman do?

A. She'll buy the bicycle.

B. She'll take a look at the bicycle.

C. She'll leave the store.

* *on sale* 特價；拍賣　　*take a look at* 看一看

23. (**B**) M：What kind of TV programs do you like?

W：Talk shows. I like them a lot. Do you like them?

M：No, I don't like them very much. I like soap operas.

Question：What kind of TV programs does the
woman like?

A. Game shows.

B. Talk shows.

C. Soap operas.

* program〔'progræm〕*n.* 節目

talk show 脫口秀（在美國相當流行的節目型態，由主持人
訪問來賓，貫串全場。）

soap〔sop〕*n.* 肥皂　　opera〔'ɑpərə〕*n.* 歌劇

soap opera 連續劇（俗稱肥皂劇）

game show 益智節目

24. (**C**) M：What time is it?

W：It's about 4:30.

M：4:30! Already?! I didn't realize it was so late.
I need to get to the bank before it closes.

Question：Why is the man in a hurry?

A. He has to catch a train.

B. He needs to be home in time for dinner.

C. He has to go to the bank.

* realize〔'riə,laɪz〕*v.* 了解　　***in a hurry*** 匆忙

catch a train 趕火車　　***in time*** 及時

25. (**C**)　M：Amy is an awful singer!
　　　　　　W：I agree.　Her voice is so loud!
　　　　　　M：And her singing's off key!
　　　　　　W：I feel the same way.

　　　　　Question：According to the speakers, how does
　　　　　　　　　　Amy sing?

　　　　　A. Wonderfully.
　　　　　B. So-so.
　　　　　C. Terribly.

　　　　＊ awful (ˈɔfl̩) *adj.* 可怕的；很糟的
　　　　　 agree (əˈgri) *v.* 同意　　voice (vɔɪs) *n.* 聲音
　　　　　 key (ki) *n.* 音調　　*sing off key* 唱歌走音
　　　　　I feel the same way. 我也這樣覺得。(= *I agree.*)
　　　　　according to 根據
　　　　　 wonderfully (ˈwʌndəfəlɪ) *adv.* 很棒地
　　　　　 so-so (ˈso,so) *adj.* 不好不壞的；馬馬虎虎的
　　　　　 terribly (ˈtɛrəblɪ) *adv.* 可怕地；很糟地

26. (**A**)　M：Hello.
　　　　　　W：Hello.　Is Ricky there?
　　　　　　M：There is no such person here.　I'm afraid you
　　　　　　　　have the wrong number.

　　　　　Question：What did the woman do?

　　　　　A. She dialed the wrong number.
　　　　　B. She talked to Ricky.
　　　　　C. She lied to Ricky.

　　　　＊ dial (ˈdaɪəl) *v.* 撥（電話號碼）　　　lie (laɪ) *v.* 說謊

27. (**C**) M : Thank you for inviting me. The dinner was delicious!

W : You're welcome. I'm glad you enjoyed it. Please come again.

M : Thanks, I'd love to! Good-bye!

W : Good-bye! Drive carefully!

Question : What did they do in the evening?

A. They went to a great movie.

B. They went shopping.

C. They had a wonderful meal.

* invite (ɪn'vaɪt) v. 邀請
  You're welcome. 不客氣。（當別人道謝時的回答。）
  meal (mil) n. 一餐

28. (**B**) M : I'd like a bottle of vitamin E.

W : Sure. Here you are. Anything else?

M : I'd also like something for a cold.

W : OK. Let me get that for you.

Question : Where are the speakers?

A. At a bookstore.

B. At a drugstore.

C. At a restaurant.

* bottle ('batḷ) n. 瓶子　　vitamin ('vaɪtəmɪn) n. 維他命
  Here you are. 你要的東西在這裡；拿去吧。
  cold (kold) n. 感冒
  drugstore ('drʌg,stor) n. 藥房

29. (**C**) M : Are you going to go to the library tonight?

W : No, I'm too tired. I want to go to bed early.

Question : What does the woman mean?

A. She's so tired that she'll go to the library.

B. She's tired enough to go to the library.

C. She's too tired to go to the library.

* ***so…that~*** 太…以致於~　　***…enough to~*** 夠…足以~

too…to~ 太…以致於不~

30. (**C**) M : May I speak to Mr. Brown?

W : He is out. Just a minute, I heard him coming in.

M : Oh, I'm lucky.

Question : What will the man do?

A. Leave a message.

B. Go out.

C. Talk with Mr. Brown.

* ***Just a minute.*** 請等一下。　　lucky〔ˈlʌkɪ〕*adj.* 幸運的

message〔ˈmɛsɪdʒ〕*n.* 訊息；留言

leave a message 留言

─【劉毅老師的話】─────

「學習出版公司」專門出版學英文的書，

學英文的書，「學習」都有。你需要什麼

書，「學習」沒有，請告訴我們。

全民英語能力分級檢定測驗

初級聽力測驗⑧

　　本測驗分三部份，全爲三選一之選擇題，每部份各 10 題，共 30 題，作答時間約 20 分鐘。

第一部份：　看圖辨義

　　　　　本部份共 10 題，試題冊上每題有一個圖片，請聽錄音機播出一個相關的問題，與 A、B、C 三個英語敘述後，選一個與所看到圖片最相符的答案，並在答案紙上相對的圓圈內塗黑作答。每題播出一遍，問題及選項均不印在試題冊上。

例：（看）

NT$80　　NT$50

（聽）

Look at the picture.　How much is the hamburger?

　　A.　It's eighty dollars.
　　B.　It's fifty-five dollars.
　　C.　It's eighteen dollars.

正確答案爲 A

Question 1

Question 2

Question 3

> # SKI TRIP
>
> Come join us for a ski trip
> to Aspen. We will have lots
> of fun and fresh powder snow.
> For more information,
> contact Leo at 555-4578.

Question 4

Question 5

Question 6

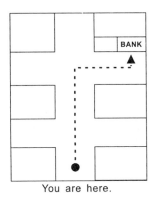

請翻頁 ⫸

Question 7

Question 8

Question 9

Question 10

請翻頁 ⫸

第二部份： 問答

本部份共 10 題，每題錄音機會播出一個問句或直述句，
每題播出一次，聽後請從試題冊上 A、B、C 三個選項中，
選出一個最適合的回答或回應，並在答案紙上塗黑作答。

例：

（聽） Good morning, Kevin. How are you?

（看） A. I'm fine, thank you.
B. I'm in the living room.
C. My name is Kevin.

正確答案爲 A

11. A. I'm eating a
hamburger.
B. I'm going home.
C. I'll go get my car.

12. A. I'm not enjoying
myself.
B. I'm not going.
C. Thank you for
inviting me.

13. A. I was reading my book.
B. I went to the
supermarket.
C. I didn't come here.

14. A. Turn left and it's on
your right.
B. Take the MRT.
C. You can ride your
bicycle to school.

15. A. Okey doke.
    B. I like cheeseburgers.
    C. It is a double bacon
       cheeseburger.

16. A. Says who?
    B. Get lost!
    C. Call me James.

17. A. Calm down.
    B. You are speaking
       now.
    C. Don't say anything.

18. A. You did.
    B. You did?
    C. You didn't?

19. A. No, it leaves at
       7:20 p.m.
    B. No, it costs 90 dollars.
    C. No, it will arrive
       tonight.

20. A. Nothing too colorful.
    B. Checkered, please.
    C. Medium, please.

請 翻 頁 ◀▯⟹

第三部份： 簡短對話

本部份共 10 題，每題錄音機會播出一段對話及一個相關
的問題，每題播出兩次，聽後請從試題冊上 A、B、C 三
個選項中，選出一個最適合的回答，並在答案紙上塗黑
作答。

例：

（聽）(Woman)　Good afternoon, …Mr. Davis?

　　　(Man)　　Yes.　I have an appointment with
　　　　　　　Dr. Sanders at two o'clock.　My
　　　　　　　son Tommy has a fever.

　　　(Woman)　Oh, that's too bad.　Well, please
　　　　　　　have a seat, Mr. Davis.　Dr.
　　　　　　　Sanders will be right with you.

　　　Question:　Where did this conversation take
　　　　　　　place?

（看）A.　In a post office.

　　　B.　In a restaurant.

　　　C.　In a doctor's office.

正確答案為 C

21. A. She thinks it's
      interesting.
    B. She thinks it's boring.
    C. She thinks it's none
      of her business.

22. A. City Hall.
    B. Bus stop.
    C. The World Trade
      Center.

23. A. She has to finish her
      reports.
    B. She has to rest.
    C. She has the flu.

24. A. He likes it.
    B. He thinks it's too
      expensive.
    C. He likes the other
      kind.

25. A. After dinner.
    B. Before dinner.
    C. He will forget.

26. A. He bought it.
    B. Someone gave it to
      him.
    C. The woman gave it
      to him.

27. A. The deer.
    B. The front yard.
    C. The flowers.

28. A. He lost his kitten.
    B. He climbed a ladder.
    C. He broke his leg.

29. A. He likes the song.
    B. He likes the woman.
    C. He doesn't like the
      song.

30. A. The man bought it
      for her.
    B. Her father bought it
      for her.
    C. An old man bought
      it for her.

初級聽力測驗詳解⑧

第一部份

Look at the picture for question 1.

1. (**A**) What are they doing?
   A. They are playing basketball.
   B. They are playing baseball.
   C. They are playing softball.

   * basketball (ˈbæskɪtˌbɔl) n. 籃球
     baseball (ˈbesˈbɔl) n. 棒球
     softball (ˈsɔftˌbɔl) n. 壘球

Look at the picture for question 2.

2. (**B**) What is the girl doing?
   A. She is skiing.
   B. She is skating.
   C. She is dancing.

   * ski (ski) v. 滑雪   skate (sket) v. 溜冰

Look at the picture for question 3.

3. (**B**) What is this a notice of?
   A. A party.
   B. A trip.
   C. A meeting.

   * notice (ˈnotɪs) n. 公告；通知
     meeting (ˈmitɪŋ) n. 會議

Look at the picture for question 4.

4. (**C**) What is Tom doing?

    A. He is sitting down.

    B. He is holding a stick.

    C. He is fishing.

    * hold〔hold〕*v.* 握住；拿著
      stick〔stɪk〕*n.* 棍子　　fish〔fɪʃ〕*v.* 釣魚

Look at the picture for question 5.

5. (**A**) What will Mary do after lunch?

    A. She will take a nap.

    B. She will do her homework.

    C. She will go shopping.

    * nap〔næp〕*n.* 小睡　　***take a nap*** 小睡
      go shopping 去購物

Look at the picture for question 6.

6. (**B**) How do I get to the bank?

    A. Turn right and turn left and stay left.

    B. Turn right at the second street, then you'll see it on your left.

    C. Turn right at the second street, then you'll see it on your right.

    * right〔raɪt〕*adv.* 向右方；在右邊　*n.* 右邊
      left〔lɛft〕*adv.* 向左方；在左邊　*n.* 左邊
      stay〔ste〕*v.* 維持；停留

Look at the picture for question 7.

7. (**C**) What is Jim cooking?
   A. He is cooking hamburgers.
   B. He is cooking steak.
   C. He is cooking bacon.

   * steak〔stek〕*n.* 牛排　　bacon〔'bekən〕*n.* 培根

Look at the picture for question 8.

8. (**C**) How many fish did Jason catch?
   A. 3.
   B. 2.
   C. 5.

   * fish〔fɪʃ〕*n.* 魚　　catch〔kætʃ〕*v.* 捕捉

Look at the picture for question 9.

9. (**A**) What is Jenny doing?
   A. She is playing the piano.
   B. She is playing the horn.
   C. She is playing the drums.

   * *play the piano* 彈鋼琴　　horn〔hɔrn〕*n.* 喇叭
   play the horn 吹喇叭　　drum〔drʌm〕*n.* 鼓
   play the drums 打鼓

Look at the picture for question 10.

10. (**C**) Where are they going?

      A. They are going to the airplane.

      B. They are going to the airport.

      C. They are going to Japan.

      * airplane ('ɛr͵plen) *n.* 飛機 (= *plane*)

      airport ('ɛr͵port) *n.* 機場

      Japan (dʒə'pæn) *n.* 日本

第二部份

11. (**B**) Stop! Where are you going?

      A. I'm eating a hamburger.

      B. I'm going home.

      C. I'll go get my car.

      * ***I'll go get my car.*** 我要去開車。(= *I'll go and get my car.*)

12. (**C**) Thank you very much for coming. I hope you will enjoy yourself.

      A. I'm not enjoying myself.

      B. I'm not going.

      C. Thank you for inviting me.

      * ***enjoy*** *oneself* 玩得愉快 (= *have a good time* = *have fun*)

      invite (ɪn'vaɪt) *v.* 邀請

13. (**B**) You're late. Where did you go?
   A. I was reading my book.
   B. I went to the supermarket.
   C. I didn't come here.

   * late〔let〕*adj.* 遲到的
     supermarket〔'supɚ͵mɑrkɪt〕*n.* 超級市場

14. (**A**) How can I get to the MRT station?
   A. Turn left and it's on your right.
   B. Take the MRT.
   C. You can ride your bicycle to school.

   * ***get to*** 到達　***MRT*** 捷運 (= *Mass Rapid Transit*)
     turn left 左轉　right〔raɪt〕*n.* 右邊

15. (**A**) Let's go get some hamburgers. I'm hungry.
   A. Okey doke.
   B. I like cheeseburgers.
   C. It is a double bacon cheeseburger.

   * ***go get*** 去買 (= *go and get*)
     okey doke〔'okɪ'dok〕*adj.* (俚) 好的
      (= *O.K.* = *okay* = *okey dokey*〔'okɪ'dokɪ〕)
     cheeseburger〔'tʃiz͵bɝgɚ〕*n.* 起士漢堡
     double〔'dʌbḷ〕*adj.* 雙層的
     bacon〔'bekən〕*n.* 培根

16. (**C**) What's your name?
   A. Says who?
   B. Get lost!
   C. Call me James.

   * ***Says who?*** 誰說的？　***Get lost!*** 滾開！

17. (**A**) I'm so mad that I can't speak.
  A. Calm down.
  B. You are speaking now.
  C. Don't say anything.

  * *so…that*~ 如此…以致於~　　mad〔mæd〕*adj.* 生氣的
  calm down 冷靜下來

18. (**B**) I finally made it. I barely caught the train.
  A. You did.
  B. You did?
  C. You didn't?

  * finally〔'faɪnḷɪ〕*adv.* 最後　　*make it* 成功；做到
  barely〔'bɛrlɪ〕*adv.* 幾乎不　　catch〔kætʃ〕*v.* 趕上

19. (**A**) The train leaves at 7:00 p.m., doesn't it?
  A. No, it leaves at 7:20 p.m.
  B. No, it costs 90 dollars.
  C. No, it will arrive tonight.

20. (**C**) What size shirt do you wear?
  A. Nothing too colorful.
  B. Checkered, please.
  C. Medium, please.

  * shirt〔ʃɜt〕*n.* 襯衫
  colorful〔'kʌləfəl〕*adj.* 顏色鮮豔的
  checkered〔'tʃɛkəd〕*adj.* 有不同顏色方格子圖案的
  medium〔'midɪəm〕*adj.* 中等的；尺寸 M 的

第三部份

21. (**B**) W : What do you do all day?

M : I work in an office. I type up reports all day and go to meetings.

W : That sounds boring.

Question : What does the woman think of the man's job?

A. She thinks it's interesting.

B. She thinks it's boring.

C. She thinks it's none of her business.

* ***all day*** 整天　　office〔'ɔfɪs〕*n.* 辦公室
type up 把～打字成文　　meeting〔'mitɪŋ〕*n.* 會議
boring〔'borɪŋ〕*adj.* 無聊的　　***think of*** 認爲
interesting〔'ɪntrɪstɪŋ〕*adj.* 有趣的
none of *one's* ***business*** 不關某人的事

22. (**C**) W : Excuse me, how do I get to the World Trade Center?

M : Take the number 2 bus and get off at the City Hall stop. Then walk 2 blocks past the City Hall. You can't miss it.

W : Thanks a lot.

Question : Where does the woman want to go?

A. City Hall.

B. Bus stop.

C. The World Trade Center.

* ***get to*** 到達　　***World Trade Center*** 世貿中心
get off 下車　　***City Hall*** 市政府
stop〔stɑp〕*n.* 站牌　　block〔blɑk〕*n.* 街區
past〔pæst〕*prep.* 經過　　miss〔mɪs〕*v.* 錯過

23. (**A**)　M：You don't look so good.　Maybe you ought to take the rest of the day off.

　　　W：I can't.　I have to finish these reports.

　　　M：Well, be sure to get plenty of rest tonight.

　　Question：Why can't the woman go home?

　　A. She has to finish her reports.

　　B. She has to rest.

　　C. She has the flu.

　　* **ought to** 應該（= *should*）　　**take ~ off** 休息~
　　　rest〔rɛst〕*n.* 其餘；休息　*v.* 休息
　　　report〔rɪˈport〕*n.* 報告
　　　plenty of 許多　　flu〔flu〕*n.* 流行性感冒

24. (**B**)　M：Excuse me, ma'am.　How much is this hat?

　　　W：That one is $59.99.

　　　M：Wow!　That's a little steep.

　　　W：We have this other kind on sale.　I think you'll like it.

　　Question：What does the man think of the hat?

　　A. He likes it.

　　B. He thinks it's too expensive.

　　C. He likes the other kind.

　　* **a little** 有一點　　steep〔stip〕*adj.* 陡的；昂貴的
　　　kind〔kaɪnd〕*n.* 種類　　**on sale** 特價；拍賣

25. (**A**) W：Did you pick up the mail?

M：Not yet. I thought I'd pick it up after dinner.

W：OK. Don't forget.

Question：When will the man pick up the mail?

A. After dinner.

B. Before dinner.

C. He will forget.

* ***pick up*** 拿取　　mail〔mel〕*n.* 郵件

26. (**B**) W：Where did you get that tie? It's terrible.

M：Well, I got it for my birthday.

Question：How did the man get the tie?

A. He bought it.

B. Someone gave it to him.

C. The woman gave it to him.

* tie〔taɪ〕*n.* 領帶　　terrible〔'tɛrəbḷ〕*adj.* 很糟的

27. (**C**) M：Hey, look! There's a deer in our front yard.

W：Wait a minute! It's eating my flowers.

M：Don't worry. I'll go chase him off.

Question：What is the woman worried about?

A. The deer.

B. The front yard.

C. The flowers.

* deer〔dɪr〕*n.* 鹿　　***front yard*** 前院

chase〔tʃes〕*v.* 追趕　　***be worried about*** 擔心

28. (**C**) M : I heard Tom fell off a ladder and broke his leg yesterday.

W : No way! What was he doing on a ladder anyway?

M : I guess he was trying to save his kitten.

W : I hope he gets well soon.

Question : What happened to Tom?

A. He lost his kitten.

B. He climbed a ladder.

C. He broke his leg.

* ***fall off*** 從～跌落　　ladder〔'lædɚ〕 *n.* 梯子
break〔brek〕*v.* 折斷；跌斷　　***no way*** 不可能
anyway〔'ɛnɪˌwe〕 *adv.* 不管怎麼說；無論如何
guess〔gɛs〕*v.* 猜　　save〔sev〕*v.* 救
kitten〔'kɪtn̩〕 *n.* 小貓　　***get well*** 康復
climb〔klaɪm〕*v.* 爬

29. (**A**) W : Can you turn down the music? It's getting on my nerves.

M : But this is a great song.

W : I don't care. Just turn it down.

Question : Why won't the man turn down the music?

A. He likes the song.

B. He likes the woman.

C. He doesn't like the song.

* ***turn down*** 關小聲　　***get on*** one's ***nerves*** 令某人心煩
care〔kɛr〕*v.* 在乎

30. (**B**)　M：Wow! Check out the new ride. When did you
　　　　　　 get this?

　　　　 W：My old man bought it for me last week. I'd like a
　　　　　　 beamer personally, but I guess a Mercedes will do.

　　　　 M：Let's go for a ride.

　　　　 W：Right on!

　　　 Question：How did the woman get the new car?

　　　 A. The man bought it for her.

　　　 B. Her father bought it for her.

　　　 C. An old man bought it for her.

* ***check out*** 查看　　　ride〔raɪd〕*n.*（俚）汽車；機車
　old man（俚）父親
　beamer〔'bimɚ〕*n.*（俚）BMW 汽車
　personally〔'pɝsn̩lɪ〕*adv.* 就自己而言；本身
　Mercedes〔mɝ'sedɪs〕*n.*（俚）賓士車
　do〔du〕*v.* 適合；好　　***go for a ride*** 開車兜風
　right on 好

劉毅英文國三基本學力測驗模考班

I. **招生對象**：國中三年級同學

II. **教學目標**：協助國三同學，順利通過「國中基本學力測驗」，和「各校第二階段甄選入學考試」。

III. **開課班級**：

英文 A 班	每週六上午 9：00~12：00	數 學 班	每週日上午 9：00~12：00
英文 C 班	每週六晚上 6：00~ 9：00	理 化 班	每週六下午 2：00~ 5：00
英文 E 班	每週日下午 2：00~ 5：00	文 科 班	每週日晚上 6：00~ 9：00

IV. **獎學金制度**：
1. 本班同學在學校班上，國二下學期或國三上學期總成績，只要有一次第一名者，可獲得獎學金 **3000** 元，第二名 **1000** 元，第三名 **1000** 元。
2. 學校模擬考試，只要有一次班上前十名，可得獎學金 **1000** 元。
3. 每次來本班考模擬考試，考得好有獎，進步也有獎，各種獎勵很多。

V. **授課內容**：
1. 本班獨創**模擬考制度**。
   根據 91 年「基本學力測驗」最新命題趨勢，蒐集命題委員參考資料，完全比照學力測驗題型編排。「基本學力測驗」得高分的秘訣，就是：**模擬考試➡上課檢討➡針對弱點加以加強**。
2. **本班掌握最新命題趨勢**：題型全為**單一選擇題**、題材以多樣化及實用性為原則。英文科加考書信、時刻表等題型；數學科則著重觀念題型，須建立基本觀念，融會貫通；理化科著重於實驗及原理運用。我們聘請知名高中學校老師（如建中、北一女、師大附中、中山、成功等），**完全按照基本學力測驗的題型命題**。
3. 每週上課前先考 50 分鐘模擬考，考後老師立即講解，馬上釐清同學錯誤的觀念。**當天考卷改完，立即發還**。

劉毅英文家教班（國一、國二、國三、高一、高二、高三班）

班址：台北市重慶南路一段 10 號 7F（捷運重慶南路出口處） ☎ (02)2381-3148・2331-8822

劉毅英文家教班 90 年國三第一次基本學力測驗榮譽榜

姓名	學校	班級	分數	姓名	學校	班級	分數	姓名	學校	班級	分數	姓名	學校	班級	分數
林日蘋	景興國中	309	60	楊若平	中正國中	320	60	蘇亭爾	蘭雅國中	303	54	盧洺霈	蘭雅國中	318	51
吳冠蓉	薇閣中學	三信	60	詹偉弘	興雅國中	314	60	林彥廷	大安國中	312	54	朱怡瑾	南門國中	304	51
牛曰正	大安國中	305	60	趙若廷	南門國中	309	60	林靖淳	大安國中	315	54	朱哲妤	蘭雅國中	320	51
呂俊樂	信義國中	318	60	劉乙萱	自強國中	312	60	林環妤	仁愛國中	315	54	朱耿宏	景美國中	304	51
李孟樺	自強國中	323	60	蔡濟謙	信義國中	318	60	邵聯安	中和國中	306	54	吳仲倫	基隆中正	302	51
李亭蓉	信義國中	313	60	顏子菁	北安國中	305	60	洪碩風	靜心中學	三忠	54	吳宜容	大安國中	302	51
李嘉霖	成淵高中	309	60	魏文耀	靜心中學	3仁	60	洪慧竹	天母國中	307	54	呂冠廷	新竹建華	三美	51
周佩璇	仁愛國中	309	60	嚴少妤	介壽國中	306	60	胡倖華	金華國中	317	54	李佩融	明德國中	308	51
周宜姍	漳和國中	304	60	蘇怡文	金華國中	311	60	范姜宛柔	弘道國中	303	54	李宛凌	興雅國中	311	51
周奎銘	格致中學	302	60	吳玉婕	木柵國中	308	60	徐偉恩	麗山國中	317	54	林千皓	金華國中	315	51
林芷帆	景美國中	305	60	吳姿儀	仁愛國中	328	60	徐維敏	中正國中	315	54	林或祥	信義國中	315	51
林颯妍	仁愛國中	328	60	易采葳	中正國中	320	60	高慧珊	聖心女中	三仁	54	林珈妤	自強國中	320	51
林煒清	增公國中	304	60	林建瑋	明德國中	322	60	張耀聰	金華國中	320	54	邱育佳	大安國中	321	51
柯佩均	金華國中	304	60	林敏珊	仁愛國中	317	60	陳文苑	金陵女中	三眞	54	侯權晏	蘭雅國中	307	51
洪彩鈞	仁愛國中	330	60	施怡安	金華國中	309	60	陳志明	二信中學	3仁	54	段佳宏	南門國中	315	51
洪嘉蔚	三和國中	307	60	唐郁善	蘭雅國中	303	54	陳怡瑗	格致中學	308	54	洪純瑀	自強國中	311	51
高啓泰	自強國中	312	60	張文翰	永平中學	301	54	陳明瑄	仁愛國中	319	54	胡涵喩	光仁國中	三和	51
張登豪	永平中學	306	60	陳美儒	景興國中	308	54	陳奕全	西松高中	301	54	翁宛婷	實踐國中	312	51
張灝	石牌國中	313	60	陳愛陵	麗山國中	302	54	陳姵含	自強國中	311	54	梁恆豪	民族國中	303	51
曹恆嘉	徐匯中學	302	60	曾品方	懷生國中	303	60	陳碩鴻	景文中學	303	54	陳佳吟	金陵女中	三樂	51
許海晨	光仁中學	三忠	60	蘇園婷	景美國中	306	54	游知箐	五常國中	310	54	陳亭春	龍山國中	302	51
連珮婷	基隆中正	305	60	王品嵐	龍山國中	301	54	黃曼婷	東山中學	三信	54	陳瑩璦	天母國中	308	51
郭士銘	蘭雅國中	320	60	王筑嫻	靜心中學	三孝	54	黃麗蓉	中山國中	306	54	陶威宇	中正國中	304	51
陳乃寧	金華國中	309	60	王瀞康	基隆中正	308	54	葉思遠	潮前國中	307	54	游婷予	光仁中學	三愛	51
陳劭瑜	中正國中	322	60	史珮琪	仁愛國中	314	54	詹涵予	中正國中	319	54	黃令宜	金陵女中	3平	51
陳怡潔	仁愛國中	315	60	刑博森	南門國中	315	54	廖怡婷	蘭雅國中	308	54	黃怡綾	建成國中	305	51
陳思穎	成淵高中	305	60	吳珮吟	蘭雅國中	303	54	廖怡婷	蘭雅國中	308	54	黃馨瑩	大安國中	308	51
陳昭霖	仁愛國中	314	60	吳珮綺	江翠國中	326	54	趙式隆	信義國中	302	54	楊淮州	自強國中	312	51
陳韋錚	金華國中	308	60	呂威辰	自強國中	313	54	劉盈蘭	士林國中	308	54	劉怡伶	介壽國中	306	51
曾敬尹	大安國中	324	60	李居榆	民權國中	310	54	蔡佳吾	石牌國中	328	54	劉家彤	北投國中	310	51
湯金翰	基隆中正	311	60	李奕萱	仁愛國中	312	54	盧佳言	信義國中	311	54	歐乃寧	東海中學	三忠	51
黃芬怡	五常國中	310	60	李祐維	信義國中	306	54	賴于彙	蘭雅國中	303	54	鄧沛宣	景興國中	315	51
黃植虹	大安國中	315	60	林凡乂	金陵女中	3平	54	簡詩芳	中正國中	322	54	鄧維元	螢橋國中	308	51
楊翔福	實踐國中	304	60	林佳伶	景興國中	308	54	謝沁輝	蘭雅國中	317	51	魯婷	大安國中	316	51
葉柏成	弘道國中	313	60	林姿君	基隆銘傳	302	54	簡志潼	自強國中	320	51	林鈺昇	金華國中	314	51
葉鈞豪	南門國中	314	60	林建治	格致中學	305	54	王育琳	忠孝國中	303	51	蔡文幸	北安國中	312	51

※「劉毅英文家教班國三班」的同學考得太好了！這次考試英文科滿分是 60 分，錯一題扣 6 分，為 54 分，錯兩題則為 51 分，錯三題則為 49 分。

劉毅英文家教班高一班招生簡章

- **開課班級：**依各校採用不同的版本，分版本分班開課。

遠東A班	週二晚上6：00～9：00	三民陳A班	週六上午9：00～12：00
遠東B班	週三晚上6：00～9：00	龍騰A班	週日上午9：00～12：00
遠東C班	週六晚上6：00～9：00	龍騰B班	週五晚上6：00～9：00
遠東D班	週日下午2：00～5：00	南　一　班	週四晚上6：00～9：00

- **課程內容：**

  1. 因應各校使用不同的版本，**劉毅英文發揮團隊力量，照顧到每一種版本的同學**，不浪費同學時間。平時上課，先考上週教的內容，檢討完，再上新的課程。只有**考試的時候，同學最專心**。一般補習班不敢考試，學生的成績不會進步，一般補習班不敢強迫學生背單字，英文一輩子都學不好。**劉毅英文嚴格要求同學背單字，效果奇佳**。

  2. 每週上課，我們會**詳盡解析課文內容**，包括單字記憶運用、文法觀念講解，以及句型變化演練等，課程安排豐富紮實，讓你收穫最多。週考部份，由本班授課老師及明星高中老師命題，內容包括聽力、會話、文意字彙、文法觀念、閱讀測驗、克漏字、翻譯等，**完全掌握月期考試題**，讓你在月期考中名列前茅。

  3. **各學校採用的課外教材**，我們將會歸納整理後，編成課外補充教材，讓同學背，或開講座課程為同學授課，真正完全照顧到同學的需要。

- **獎學金制度：**

  1. 背完第一冊單字的同學，前300名可領獎學金*1000*元，背完第二冊，前300名可再領獎學金*1000*元。

  2. 本班同學在學校班上月期考英文成績第一名，可獲得獎學金*3000*元，第二名及第三名可得*1000*元。（每人限領一次，若名次進步，可再領差額。）

  3. 本班每週週考成績、學期總成績優異同學，均有獎勵，鼓勵同學努力讀英文。

劉毅英文家教班（國一、國二、國三、高一、高二、高三班）

班址：台北市重慶南路一段10號7F（消防隊斜對面）　☎（02）2381-3148・2331-8822
網址：http://www.learnschool.com.tw

||||||||||||●學習出版公司門市部●|||||||||||||||

台北地區：台北市許昌街 10 號 2 樓 TEL：(02)2331-4060・2331-9209
台中地區：台中市綠川東街 32 號 8 樓 23 室
　　　　　TEL：(04)2223-2838

|||||||||||||||||||||||||||||||||||||||||||||

初級英語聽力檢定 ②

主　　　編 / 劉　毅
發 行 所 / 學習出版有限公司　　　☎ (02) 2704-5525
郵 撥 帳 號 / 0512727-2 學習出版社帳戶
登 記 證 / 局版台業 2179 號
印 刷 所 / 裕強彩色印刷有限公司
台 北 門 市 / 台北市許昌街 10 號 2 F　　☎ (02) 2331-4060・2331-9209
台 中 門 市 / 台中市綠川東街 32 號 8 F 23 室　　☎ (04) 2223-2838
台灣總經銷 / 紅螞蟻圖書有限公司　　☎ (02) 2795-3656
美國總經銷 / Evergreen Book Store　　☎ (818) 2813622
本公司網址　www.learnbook.com.tw
電 子 郵 件　learnbook@learnbook.com.tw

售價：新台幣一百八十元正
2003 年 3 月 1 日一版二刷

ISBN 957-519-572-8